LAST STAND AT PAPAGO WELLS

LAST STAND AT PAPAGO WELLS

LOUIS L'AMOUR

BANTAM BOOKS
NEW YORK • TORONTO • LONDON • SYDNEY • AUCKLAND

LAST STAND AT PAPAGO WELLS
*A Bantam Book / published by arrangement with
the author*

PUBLISHING HISTORY
The Louis L'Amour Hardcover Collection / July 1986

If you want to purchase more of these titles, please write to:
The Louis L' Amour Collection
1540 Broadway
New York, NY 10036

ISBN 0-553-06286-7

Published simultaneously in the United States and Canada

---

*Bantam Books are published by Bantam Books, a division of Bantam
Doubleday Dell Publishing Group, Inc. Its trademark, consisting of
the words "Bantam Books" and the portrayal of a rooster, is Registered
in U.S. Patent and Trademark Office and in other countries. Marca
Registrada. Bantam Books, 1540 Broadway, New York, New York
10036.*

PRINTED IN THE UNITED STATES OF AMERICA

0   9   8   7   6   5   4

LAST STAND AT PAPAGO WELLS

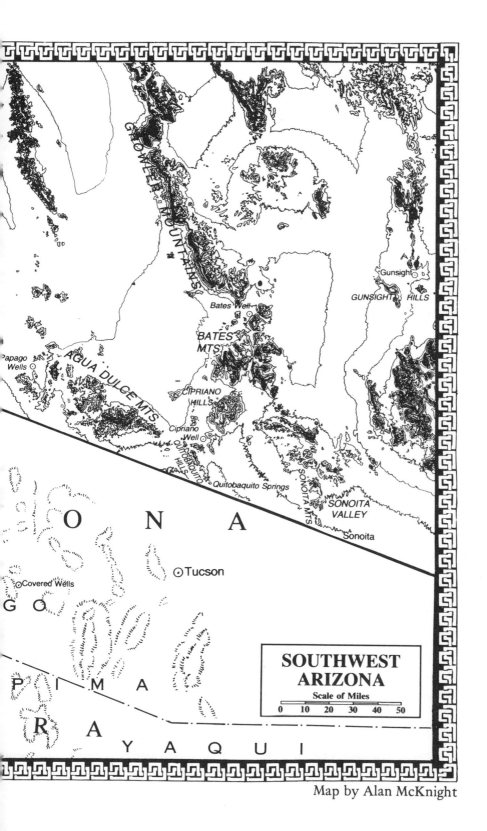

GROWLER MOUNTAINS

Gunsight

GUNSIGHT HILLS

Bates Well

BATES MTS.

Papago Wells

AGUA DULCE MTS

CIPRIANO HILLS

Cipriano Well

QUITOBAQUITO HILLS

Quitobaquito Springs

SONOITA MTS

SONOITA VALLEY

Sonoita

O N A

⊙ Tucson

⊙ Covered Wells

G O

P I M A

R A Y A Q U I

SOUTHWEST ARIZONA

Scale of Miles

0   10   20   30   40   50

Map by Alan McKnight

ONE

He had stopped last night in the Gunsight Hills, making dry camp because others had reached the water hole before him and he preferred to avoid other travelers. At daybreak he came down out of the hills and made a little dust as he struck westward with Yuma Crossing in his mind.

Logan Cates had the look of the desert about him, a brown, seasoned man with straight black hair above a triangular face that was all bone and tight-drawn, sun-browned hide. His eyes, narrow from squinting into sun and wind, were a cold green that made a man stop and think before he looked into them a second time.

He was a tall man, wide in the shoulder and lean in waist and hips, an easy-moving man with none of the horseman's awkwardness in walking. He moved like a hunter when on his own feet, and had been a hunter of many things, men not least among them.

His hat was black and flat-crowned and flat-brimmed, held beneath his jaw by a loose thong. His shirt, once red, had faded to an indeterminate rose. His vest was of black cowhide, worn and scratched, and over his black jeans he wore fringed shotgun chaps. He wore a tied-down Smith & Wesson Russian

1

LOUIS L'AMOUR

.44 six-shooter, and the Winchester in his saddle-scabbard was the vintage of '73.

The horse he rode, a long-legged zebra dun, had a wicked eye that hinted at the tough, resilient and often vicious nature within. A horse of many brands, he had the speed of a frightened coyote and an ability to go without water equal to any camel or longhorn steer.

Logan Cates was a man without illusions, without wealth, place, or destination. In the eighteen years since his parents died of cholera when he was fourteen he had driven a freight wagon, punched cows, hunted buffalo, twice gone over the trail from Texas to Kansas with cattle, scouted for the Army and had ridden shotgun on many stages. Twice, also, he had been marshal of boomtowns for brief periods. He had lived without plan, following his horse's ears and coping with each day's problems as they arose.

Not an hour out of the Gunsight Hills he drew rein in the bottom of a dry wash and crawled to the lip of the wash to survey the desert. Lifting his head among some small boulders to keep from skylining it, he studied the situation with care, having long ago learned that vigilance was the price of life in Indian country. Far away toward the line that divided Mexico from Arizona was a dust cloud.

"Ten," he judged, "maybe twelve riders."

The knowledge was disturbing, for when so many men came together in this country it spelled trouble, and no news had come his way since riding out of Tucson almost four days before. And he knew enough of the desert to the south to realize no man would ride there without desperate reason.

A dozen men could mean a posse, a band of outlaws, Indians, or any Army patrol out of Fort Yuma. The latter was highly improbable as there had been no trouble in the area for some time, and the Apaches rarely came so far west.

Yet, with Churupati in the field no dependence could be placed on that guess, for his mother had been a Yaqui, giving him ties in western Sonora.

Returning to the saddle, Logan Cates resumed his westward trek, moving more slowly and trying to lift no dust. Considering this group of riders to the south and the three who had last night stopped at Gunsight Wells the country was becoming too busy for comfort. The three at Gunsight had been too far away to distinguish details but their fire had been far larger than any Indian would build.

The trail he followed lay fifty yards off to his right, for Logan Cates had an aversion to leaving his tracks where they might be easily seen. As it was, his trail was unlikely to be found unless by riders coming into the trail from the south.

All travel in this western Arizona desert was circumscribed by the necessity for water, and the fact that in several hundred square miles there were only a few widely scattered water holes, and none of these reliable in a dry season. No matter what route a man wished to take his trail must at some time touch these water holes, for without them he would die.

Ahead of him and at least twenty miles from his camp of last night lay one of these water holes. It lay in the gap through which went the trail west, but he had been warned in Tucson that the water hole might be empty and it could in no case be depended upon. The nearest water beyond the gap was at Papago Wells on the edge of the lava beds to the south, a good twenty miles further. Unless all signs failed he would find company at one or both water holes, but there was no help for it.

This was a land of little water and less rain, where trails were indicated by the bones of men and animals that had died beside them, and all lines of travel were dictated by the urgency of water. Trails from all directions would converge on the water hole in the gap ahead of him, and if that tank proved dry then he must ride at once for Papago Wells, a grim and lonely place with its three dark pools lying in their basins of bluish-black basaltic rock.

Beyond this place the nearest water was at Tule Tank, thirty miles further on the Yuma trail, although an Indian had once told Cates of a place called Heart Tank in the Sierra Pinta

3

north of Papago Wells. Nobody else he knew had heard of Heart Tank and Cates knew how slight were the chances of finding water without adequate directions. Such a tank might exist high in the rocks as at Tinajas Altas, where men had died within a few feet of water they could not find, or who lacked the strength for the climb to its place among the high rocks.

It was very hot . . . Logan Cates squinted his eyes against the shimmering heat waves and studied the dust of the riders who had camped last night at Gunsight Wells, who were also heading due west . . . a glance to the south indicated the larger group had drawn closer, but were still distant by many miles. It would be well to ride up to Papago with a ready gun, for in this country many a man had been murdered for his horse.

Several times he drew up to study the country, uneasily aware that for this lonely desert there was too much movement.

At this moment, unknown to him, half a dozen parties of horsemen were riding toward an unexpected rendezvous at Papago Wells, and with each rode the shadow of fear, and some had already been brushed by death.

Far to the north, on another trail toward the gap, were two riders. As yet they knew nothing of those who rode south of them, and were concerned with nothing in that direction, but from time to time they turned to look along their back trail, and of the two the man showed the greater apprehension.

Tall and spare, he carried himself in the saddle as a former cavalryman should. His features were clean cut, his mustache trimmed carefully, and under the brim of his white hat his eyes were piercing blue. Unquestionably handsome, he had the appearance of a strong, purposeful man, and despite the powdering of the desert dust the black coat he wore looked trim and neat. He was a man who rode well and went armed, and the horse he rode was a splendid chestnut, bred for the Virginia hills rather than these sandy, rock-strewn wastelands. The man rode with assurance and the girl he rode beside was quick to notice it.

She was tall, her dark hair drawn back and knotted loosely,

her eyes blue-gray and large. Her every feature indicated breeding, yet there was something more than breeding or beauty in her face, there was a hint of fine steel not yet honed to a cutting edge.

"Do you think your father will follow us?"

"He'll follow."

"What will it serve if we are already married?"

"He'll kill you, I think. He's my father, but he's a brute, and I saw him kill a man once. I believe I've hated him ever since."

"Someone you knew?"

"No . . . only by sight. I had seen him around the town, and once he had come to the ranch, but he was young, gay, handsome. I quite lost my heart to him when I was ten or eleven, and then my father killed him. I never knew why."

Dust climbed around them, and the desert offered no sound but the sound of their travel. Despite the heat the girl on the gray horse looked neat, cool, perfectly composed.

She was, Grant Kimbrough decided, the best thing that had happened to him since the Civil War brought his world to an untimely end. His given name had come to him from his father, who'd fought through the Mexican War beside a grim, cigar-chewing soldier he had come to admire, and when that officer led the Union forces against the South, the elder Kimbrough saw no reason for his son to change his name. The blood of the Kimbroughs was good blood, and if there are some who say such blood wears thin with the passing generations, there was no need to say this of Grant Kimbrough at the time the war ended. He had fought well and ended the war with the rank of colonel.

His father died at Missionary Ridge and Grant returned to an impoverished estate it would take years to rebuild. His great-grandfather had begun with a wilderness, and although the land was still rich and fertile, the great-grandson elected to sell out for a song and go west.

He was a man without skills other than those expected of a gentleman. He knew how to ride, to dance, to shoot. He held

5

his liquor well and played an excellent game of cards, yet he had become accustomed to good living, and, feeling nothing could go wrong for a Kimbrough, he spent the money received for the estate freely until one morning he awakened with less than two hundred dollars and no prospects. It was then he became a professional gambler.

He began with the river-boats, then drawn by the irresistible tide that moved all things west, he proceeded from Kansas City to Ellsworth to Abilene to Dodge to Fort Worth, Cimarron and Santa Fe. On the stage to Tucson he met Jennifer Fair.

Jennifer Fair was the only child of Jim Fair, a man who knew how to build an empire on grass, how to handle men, cattle and Apaches, but never learned how to talk to his daughter, and therefore was never able to tell her how much she meant to him. His world had no place for soft words, it was abrupt, hard, dangerous and profane, and he had lived it well enough to be ranked with Pierce, Slaughter, Goodnight and Loving, those kings among cattlemen.

When Jennifer reached her father's ranch, returning from the East, she was accompanied by Grant Kimbrough. The huge, rambling old stone house reminded him of the estates of his boyhood, and he liked the simple good taste of the Spanish furniture. After the gambling halls and river-boats the great old house was subdued, peaceful, lovely.

Day after day he rode with Jennifer, talked to her and danced with her. Compared to the cowhands he was everything to delight a woman, knowing all the little courtesies and the gentleman's manner. Big Jim watched and was not pleased, but Kimbrough was his daughter's guest. And the day came when Grant Kimbrough proposed.

Jennifer had quarreled with her father over some minor subject and Grant sensed a coming break, a break he did not wish to occur. He proposed and was accepted. He approached Jim Fair with a request for his blessing and was given an hour to get off the ranch. Within the hour Grant Kimbrough was gone, but he was joined at daylight by Jennifer and together they rode to Tucson.

No priest or minister of the gospel would marry them in Tucson without Jim Fair's blessing. Coldly furious, she spent the night with a girl friend and at daybreak rode west with Grant Kimbrough and a company of people bound for Ehrenburg. From where the trails divided they would push on southwest to Yuma Crossing.

North of the gap they parted company with their companions and started south at a good clip. Grant Kimbrough knew next to nothing of southern Arizona, but there seemed to be too many moving dust clouds and they worried him. They had been pushing their horses hard when they rode into the gap and stopped at Bates Well.

Jennifer screamed.

The two men who lay sprawled in death upon the hard-packed earth had been stripped and horribly mutilated. The cracked earth in the bottom of the dry waterhole was dark with their blood. Both men had been shot through with arrows and struck many times, and about their bodies were numerous tracks of the unshod ponies of the Indians.

For the first time since he could remember, Grant Kimbrough knew fear. His soldiering experience told him these men had not long been dead, which meant the Indians might be in the vicinity even now.

"Jennifer, we've got to get away from here."

They did not hear the man who came down from the rocks behind them. He was a tall boy, shyly attractive in manner, but there was no shyness in the way he held his rifle. His clothes were shabby and when he came out of the rocks near the waterhole he cleared his throat before speaking. "You folks headed west?"

Kimbrough turned sharply, his hand automatically dropping for his gun, but when he saw the tall, slim boy who faced them he merely said, "Who're you?"

"If you folks are headed west, I'm huntin' company. My name is Lonnie Foreman."

Kimbrough gestured at the dead men. "Did you know them?"

"There were fourteen, maybe fifteen Indians. When we found the water gone I crawled up in the rocks hunting for a rock tank . . . one of these here tinajas. I was up there when the Indians came, and before I could get placed for a shot it was all over.

"We worked on a cattle outfit together, and talked it over about California. Finally we made it up to go west an' we got this far."

Jennifer had kept her eyes averted, but her heart was throbbing heavily and she kept thinking about the Indians. If there was one band out here there might be more, and she remembered stories her father had told of Indian forays. In any event, nothing was to be gained here. "We'd best go on," she said; "they might come back."

"Closest water is twenty miles . . . Papago Wells." Lonnie Foreman turned to Jennifer. "Ma'am, if you'll allow it, I'd ride with you all."

"Of course," she said.

Grant Kimbrough had started to speak, then said nothing. Another man was added protection, and boy though he might be, in this country he was a man in years as well as height. And there was something impressive about the way he handled his rifle, something casual, easy, showing long familiarity.

Due south of them was still another rock tank, this one known to Indians only and by rumor to a few prospectors and army scouts. There were Indians there now, six of them, with a recently captured white girl for prisoner.

Junie Hatchett was the last of her family. The others had died fighting in the battle after which Junie was captured. She was a prisoner now with no hope of help from any source at all. Nobody even knew she was alive, and so far as she was aware there was no one to whom it mattered. She was a thin, frightened girl with the face of a tired waif, and she held herself very still now, afraid to breathe for fear it might draw attention to her.

For a moment there was little chance of that. The Indians

were eating now, stuffing themselves on the half-raw meat of a captured mule, and when they were gorged they would sleep, and then Junie intended to escape. She knew just how she would do it, and she knew too, she would probably die in the desert.

Cipriano Well was ten miles from Bates Well in the gap through which the trail passed, and she knew it was at least twenty miles further to Papago Wells, but she would attempt to reach it. There was nearly always water there, and there were rocks in which to hide. Sooner or later someone would come.

Junie had never been to Papago Wells, but she had listened to the scout who guided their small bunch of wagons, and he had talked to them about it. She knew also that she would not live out tomorrow. When the half-starved Indians awakened after eating she would be raped and killed. She knew very well they would kill her because this was a war party and they were not returning to their homes in Mexico yet. She would be excess baggage when they were through with her.

Holding her thin body very tight and still, she watched the Indians, and waited, and hoped.

Only a few miles away the lone rider on the zebra dun paused briefly and rinsed his horse's mouth with water. He had come prepared for trouble with two large canteens, and with luck he would reach Papago Wells shortly after sundown.

Logan Cates mounted again and pushed out into the desert, riding west.

TWO

The water holes that were Papago Wells lay now as they had lain these thousands of years, resting easily in their hollow hands of rocks. Born of the earth's travail, the arroyo in which lay the three tanks had come into being amid the shattering thunder of rock, the uplifting and rending of a vertebra of the continental spine.

Later, Pinacate had come into being, spewing lava in a hot, steaming, inexorable flood over all that land that lay between Papago Wells and the Gulf of California, creating a minor hell here in this lost corner of the land. Dead volcano cones remain where they died when the fires cooled, and here and there among the fields of lava are deep craters, sunk hundreds of feet into the earth, their floors paraded with cacti just as the lava fields are starred with cholla, bisnaga and ocotillo.

This was a lonely land, rent and torn by earthquakes, its surface cracked and shattered into deep arroyos or broken blisters of lava in whose basins there was sometimes water. At Papago Wells the water lay in three smooth rock basins, sheltered in part from the sun, the water crystal clear, cool and sweet, known to few except for Indians and the few wandering animals or birds who came to this sun-baked desert.

10

In an age long gone there had been greater rainfall and then the rock basins were always full, and then the last of the great reptiles came to drink, and the first of the mammals. After the glaciers retreated in that country to the north, the rainfall became less and less, the land dried out, and much of the grass disappeared.

There was further rending of rock, further volcanic eruption, and the last of the reptiles vanished, a few lingering on to color the legends of the Indians who came drifting down from the north. Yet much remained to tell of the passing of both reptile and mammal. Deep under the sand not far from the wells lay the skull and bones of a saber-toothed cat, and nearer still, the bones of a giant sloth. A quarter of a mile away two mammoths had been trapped in a cienaga by primitive men and killed there by great rocks thrown down upon them, and then eaten.

Seven thousand years ago a man had come to drink, the first of the hunters and food gatherers to find this remote place. He knelt to drink, unaware that another hunter, the saber-toothed cat, crouched in the dead lava behind him. The primitive man carried a hand-ax of stone and a throwing stick with a spear. He heard the cat when it moved behind him and turned in time to make a thrust that tore the cat's flesh. The spear-head broke off and fell into the sand, and the man struck his dying blow with a flint knife. The cat dragged the man some fifty yards before he dropped him, and then died himself, but the spear-head remains, only a few inches under the sand west of the waterhole's edge.

Few travelers came so far south, and they came only of necessity. In normal times there was water to the north, and in this area of some hundreds of square miles what water there was would be found in catch basins from infrequent rains. Any traveler headed into this country did so at his own risk.

Sweet, clear water lay in a large pool at Papago Wells, water several feet deep and shadowed by walls of lava. Back of the main pool was another rock basin, smaller, more confined, with abrupt rock nearly enclosing it, while below the main tank

11

was another, scattered with boulders. In the arroyo below and near this tank was a dense thicket of ironwood, mesquite, palo verde and cat claw.

Rain had worn the rocks smooth, had cascaded over them in heavy storms, polishing them like glass, and in all the wilderness around there was nothing offering such water as this. Bighorn sheep came here to water, prowling mountain lions, occasional jaguar, coyote and antelope. Men came more seldom, rarely stopped for long.

To desert men and animals alike, Papago Wells offered the surest chance for water in many miles, the cool dark tanks, the arroyo with its limited shade, the galleta grass . . . it was a place not to be forgotten. Bates Well was dry, Cipriano held little water, Gunsight was a long way behind, the Tule Wells a long way ahead.

Far to the south, moving north and west now, rode a band of dark riders. Churupati, half-Apache, half-Yaqui, and all savage, was their leader. Accepted by neither tribe, from each he drew malcontents, denied by their own people, hating the white man, living only for murder and rapine. Skirting the Manteca and Espuma hills of northern Sonora they rode steadily westward, twenty-three rogue Apaches, riding toward a rendezvous with several smaller bands, to meet on the Sonoita. Scattered to their north were a few isolated ranches or mining claims, occasional Papago or Pima Indians . . . and the latter were ancient enemies. A swift foray across the border, murder, loot and burning, then they'd lose themselves in the deserts where they now traveled.

Churupati was a dark, squat man of Herculean strength, flat of nose, scarred of face, living only to kill. Swinging south he struck swiftly at Quitovac where half a dozen Mexicans worked a mine, then north for a quick raid on the horse herds at Quitobaquito, and westward to Papago Wells. At Quitovac he left five of six Mexicans dead, believing he had killed them all, then drove off the mules for feasting at Sonoita. Unknown to him he left behind at Quitovac one Mexican alive, a white man and white woman . . . he also left sixty thousand dollars in gold.

Through the desert Churupati and his men moved like shadowy brown ghosts, and always there lay in the back of Churupati's mind a memory of the still, cold waters of Papago Wells.

The water hole lay silent and alone, shaded from the desert sun. In the ironwood thicket below, a quail called. There was no other sound.

A bighorn ram led his flock to drink, dipping their muzzles in the cold, dark water after the sun went down. They were still there, enjoying their proximity to water, when they heard the click of a hoof on stone, still some distance off. Like so many shadows the bighorns vanished into the maze of lava boulders and behind them the pools looked shy and innocent under the wide, white moon.

A saddle creaked, nearer now, and two men came in from the west, conversing in low tones. "We're safe enough, Tony. If the sheriff does follow us out of Yuma he'll stay on the trail to Gunsight, then on through Covered Wells and Indian Oasis."

Tony Lugo was unconvinced. "This Yaqui country," he said.

"You Pimas are all scared of Yaquis," Jim Beaupre said. "Never saw it to fail."

Lugo shrugged. "Pima fight Yaqui many times, and Pima win, usually."

Tony Lugo was not one to harry a subject. He had said his word and he let it remain so. If Jim Beaupre wanted to stop at Papago Wells, all right. The sheriff in Yuma was a determined man and the tall boy they had killed in Yuma was his nephew. The fight had been fair enough and the boys had started it, the nephew and two companions, hunting a reputation. They were young, but even so they should have known better, and when they jumped the two strangers it was with careless contempt and the desire to be known as having killed their man.

Beaupre was an old buffalo skinner, dour, tough, weather-beaten, a man with a tang of salty humor in him and a wicked hand with a Bowie knife. Veteran of fifty Indian battles and twice that many hand-to-hand fights, he merely looked old, cantankerous and down-at-heel. Lugo—well, the half-breed had scouted for the Army, had stolen horses from the Apache and Hualapai, had done his share of fighting wherever he encountered it. Neither man wanted trouble, but the boys did. Three of them, two nineteen and one just turned twenty, and they believed they had chosen some old fool of a prospector and a harmless Indian. Now one of the boys lay dead, another had lost an arm, the third was close to death but might recover, with care.

The moon was bright on the waters of Papago Wells when they stepped down from their saddles. Men and horses drank, then retired to the thicket below, a little too wise to remain close to water where other men might come, yet knowing enough to not go too far away, nor to build a fire. In the meantime their horses could graze on galleta grass or tornillo beans, and Beaupre and Lugo would be seeing anyone who came to the Wells for water.

What Beaupre did not guess was that many would come to the Wells, and not so many would leave. Perhaps in some dark, secret convolution of his subconscious the half-breed knew it, but he had said what he had to say and it was enough to have spoken. What would be, would be.

To the south and east of Papago Wells, the party of twelve riders seen by Logan Cates had decided to turn north. The decision, taken suddenly, was as suddenly fatal.

A party of renegade Indians, headed for the rendezvous on the Sonoita, was awaiting them in a shallow wash. When the twelve riders appeared, dozing in the saddle, weary from their long ride, hot from the desert sun, the Indians opened fire. It was point-blank range, at a distance of no more than forty yards, and their first volley emptied four saddles, stampeded the horses and broke up the group.

This group was the sheriff's posse out of Yuma, and after that first savage volley they never reorganized. It had smashed destruction upon them at the end of a hot, dusty day when they were half asleep. Hunting two running men as they were, they had no idea they were themselves hunted. The sheriff himself was riding a half-tamed bronco, and before he got his horse stopped he was four miles away and all alone.

Behind him there was scattered shooting, and he had an idea little of it was being done by his own men. The nearest water was at Gunsight Wells, and he hesitated whether to try for it or to return, and when he started again the bronc caved under him. For the first time he realized his horse had been shot.

Alone then, the sheriff thought of his wife in Yuma. He knew enough of the desert to know how small were his chances of survival, but he had courage. He swore softly, realizing what those three reckless youngsters had cost, and then he began to walk. The following afternoon, still many miles from Gunsight Wells, his tongue swollen and his eyes glazed, he shot himself.

The Indians had been successful. There had been but nine Indians, and they had cut the posse in half. After the first smashing volley they had killed another man, and the sheriff, unknown to them, had been added to the list. Four of the six who survived were soldiers from Fort Yuma under the command of a veteran Irish sergeant, and these alone held together, rolled into a shallow place in the desert, and opened fire.

A fight with disciplined soldiery had no place in the Indian plans, so they slipped away to the south and Sergeant Sheehan gathered what ammunition was left on the slain men and horses, and with what canteens they could find and two recaptured horses for the extra weight, they started west. The following afternoon they were joined by the one remaining civilian, a man named Taylor, who had also kept his horse. Of the twelve these six remained.

The soldiers were of a small patrol sent out to report the condition of water holes along this route to Tucson, and they had joined the sheriff on his return toward Yuma. That the move had been a fatal one Sergeant Timothy Sheehan would be the first to confess.

Their situation was now serious. It was Sheehan's duty to report the outbreak to the post at Yuma at the earliest possible moment, but he could not spare a horse for a messenger. Their very survival might depend on the horses to carry canteens and ammunition, and later they might have to share them, turn and turn about. Their one chance for survival lay in a safe arrival at Papago Wells.

Once there they could rest, supply themselves with fresh water and make the attempt to reach Yuma. The worst of their journey undoubtedly lay between their present position and Papago. The Indians had escaped and might be returning in force, and not for one minute did Sheehan believe the few who attacked them were the only hostiles.

And so, from various points on that southern desert, parties of men on foot and horseback moved toward Papago Wells, drawn by the common necessity of water.

At Cipriano Well the Indians, gorged on mule meat, grunted in their sleep. Junie Hatchett slid the loop of her bound wrists down over her narrow hips and down behind her ankles. Then, doubling her knees under her chin, she put her bound feet through the circle of her arms and brought her wrists up in front of her. Then she began to fight the rawhide knots with her teeth.

After more than an hour of heartbreaking struggle her wrists were free, and it required half again that long to free her ankles. Ghostlike in the silence, she got up. It was impossible to get a horse, for they would be frightened of the smell of the white man about her, and the Indians would awaken. She wasted no time except to retrieve a water-bag, but walked silently away into the darkness.

Junie Hatchett was fifteen, soon to be sixteen, and her years had known little of love, much of loneliness, of longing, and of hardship. They had been years, too, of empty yearning toward the impossible . . . but from that yearning she now drew strength, for there is no power greater than the power of a dream, and she walked steadily away into the vast and empty desert, unafraid.

16

THREE

In the first gray light of day three riders rode up to Papago Wells. Jennifer Fair had all she could do to hold herself in the saddle, but exhausted as she was, there was no relenting in her purpose. Kimbrough, though disliking the presence of Lonnie Foreman, was unable to do anything about it, and had decided at last that it was just as well.

There was no wedding ring on the lady's finger, but Lonnie knew a lady when he saw one, and in his book of rules, which was strict, Jennifer Fair was a lady.

Fair . . . Jennifer Fair . . . *Big Jim Fair!*

Of course! All at once it made sense, for the name of Jim Fair was known wherever cattlemen gathered. If Jim Fair's daughter was riding out of the country with a man it was because her father disapproved of the man. Lonnie himself was a romantic, and if Jennifer loved the man, then her father had no right to object. Well . . . not much.

Lonnie Foreman knew that Grant Kimbrough was a gentleman. From the West Virginia hills himself, he knew Kimbrough for what he was at first glance—Southern aristocracy. Back where he came from there was little of that, though down in the lowlands it was quite a thing. Up where Lonnie came from a man was judged by his shooting and his farming, and

17

Lonnie had carried a rifle ever since he was tall enough to keep both ends off the ground. And he knew how to use one, too.

They had arrived on the morning after the arrival of Beaupre and Lugo, of whom they saw nothing. On this same morning, far to the east of them, Junie Hatchett walked steadily toward the west, and behind her the sleeping Indians had not yet awakened.

They had drawn up, well back from the tanks. "Maybe," Lonnie suggested in a low voice, "I better ride up and take a look. Might be Indians."

Jennifer moved to protest, but Grant Kimbrough said, "All right . . . but be careful."

Jennifer glanced at him sharply, but made no comment. Kimbrough moved his horse near hers. "The boy is good at this," he said, "we might as well let him do it."

She made no reply. The moon, in these last hours of night, had turned the cholla into torches of captured moonlight. She listened. Somewhere a pebble rattled on the rocks up ahead of them where Lonnie had gone, and a low wind stirred the desert, causing the greasewood beside them to hum faintly. It *was* beautiful . . . but so lonely, so empty. After the cities, the parties, the gaiety, the lights . . . no, this was not for her, despite the stillness, despite the beauty.

She had hated the loneliness of the ranch without women of her own kind, she detested her father's brusque good nature and his clumsy efforts to be affectionate. She hated the gun he was never without, and the memory of the gay, laughing boy it had destroyed.

The desert, she told herself, was not for women. It dried them out and burned them up, and she was glad she was getting out of it, and fortunate to have met a man like Grant Kimbrough at such a time. He was so obviously a gentleman. He had breeding . . .

Lonnie Foreman appeared in the vague light. "It's all right. Nobody around, and plenty of water. Down in the lower wash there's feed for the horses."

The feeble lemon light over the eastern mountains wid-

18

ened with the hours and crimson began to tint the far-off hills. Here and there the red dripped over and ran down a ridge into the desert. Tired as she was, Jennifer led her horse to the lower pool and stood by while he drank deep of the cool water. It was a lesson learned from her father, learned long ago.

"We'll have to rest," Kimbrough said reluctantly. "Our horses are in bad shape."

"It's a place to fight from." Foreman squatted on his heels. "We could do much worse."

Kimbrough's thoroughbred was showing the rough travel. He looked gaunt and hollow-eyed from the unaccustomed heat and dryness. Jennifer was shocked at its appearance, for her own horse, while very tired, was standing up well.

Above the pool among the lava rocks a head lifted slowly and eyes looked down upon them. It was a ragged-looking black head, and the eyes were black, Indian, curious. The watcher studied each of them in turn, remaining longer on Jennifer. To his right another head lifted and Jim Beaupre joined Lugo in sizing up the arrivals. His shrewd eyes noted with approval that the boy had not put down his rifle.

Neither man looked like the law, but there was no reason why they should be here, at this lonely place. "All right," Beaupre whispered, "we'll filter in on 'em, but take it easy. That youngster looks like he'd shoot first and ask his questions of the corpse."

Foreman got to his feet. "I've some coffee, ma'am, and I reckon we could trust a fire if we keep it small and down in the hollow. I figure to make one that won't show smoke."

"Would you, Lonnie?" Her smile was quick and friendly, and he grinned in reply. "You make the fire and I'll make the coffee."

He was returning with his arms full of wood when he saw the two men. Lonnie stopped where he was, his eyes going from one to the other, and then to his rifle, a good ten paces away. His six-shooter was in his belt but he would have to drop the wood first and he was no hand with a short gun.

19

"No call to get stirred up," Beaupre said. "We're travelin' east, an' just stopped the night."

Kimbrough turned at the sound of the voice and Lonnie saw how his coat was drawn back and that he wore his coat for a fast draw. Lonnie glanced at him sharply, finding something surprising in the gun. He had taken Kimbrough for a man just out from the East . . . he was not brown enough for a Westerner, but he wore his gun like a man who knew how to use it. Lonnie walked to where the fire would be and dropped his armful of wood.

"You better think again before you go east," Lonnie advised. " 'Paches killed my two partners at Bates Well."

"We'll wait, then." Beaupre grinned at the boy. "If they come thisaway we can stand 'em off."

"They'll come."

They built the fire under an overhang of rock where the flames could not reflect upward, although the sky was too light now to show any reflection. Over their coffee they huddled together, each busy with his or her own thoughts. Somewhere behind them, Jennifer thought, would be her father, probably with a dozen men, searching for her . . . and somewhere to the east, perhaps near him, were the Indians.

Jim Beaupre had his own thoughts and they were not attractive. A sheriff's posse was on his trail with hanging on their minds, and even if he were taken back for trial, a possibility which he did not consider likely, it would be doubtful if anyone on the jury would give them a break. Hometown folks were apt to consider such youngsters just harum-scarum boys, not giving due thought to the fact that the guns they carried were fully aged. A drifting buffalo skinner and a half-breed could expect no breaks.

From time to time Lugo slipped away from the fire to study the surrounding country. The Pima was a good man, and could see things on the desert that only an Indian would see . . . an Indian or a man who had lived there as long.

The sun was just about to tip its eyebrows over the mountain when he called down. "Man coming . . . riding alone."

20

From the shelter of the rocks they saw the man on the zebra dun. The horse had a fast, shuffling trot and he came on fast, but circling as he came, taking advantage of every bit of cover. At times they saw him, then they did not, but Jim Beaupre muttered something to Lugo, then chuckled. "He's a smart one! Right now he knows exactly where we are, and I bet he knows how many there are! He also knows what shape our horses are in . . . see him cuttin' for sign a while back?"

"He's not very intelligent," Grant Kimbrough said. "From here I could drop him at any time."

"Maybe, but don't try it. Notice how his rifle lays? My guess is he saw us as soon as we saw him and if you started to lift a gun you'd be combin' lead out of your hair. Right now he's just makin' sure this isn't a trap. I'll lay you an even dollar he gets off on the far side of his horse from where we stand."

The rider on the dun walked the horse up through the brush and they went down to meet him. Kimbrough was in the lead, and when the dun stopped walking, the Winchester lay across the pommel with the muzzle centered on Kimbrough's chest.

"How's for some coffee?" Logan Cates asked pleasantly. "I could smell it a quarter of a mile 'way."

"Come on in," Kimbrough invited, and Cates swung down, his horse between them, the rifle always ready without being obtrusive. When he was on the ground, Cates led the dun into the trees and after a minute came toward them, carrying his rifle in one hand, his canteens and saddlebags in the other.

"Picked up a smoke at daybreak," he told them, "and heard shooting off to the south."

Cates's eyes met Jennifer's and slanted away. He accepted the coffee she offered him, aware of Beaupre's quick glance at the way he wore his gun, and the longer look at his face.

As he sipped his coffee, Logan Cates tried to make sense of the little group he had joined. That the two parties had arrived separately, he was well aware, but he did not know which was which. Obviously the exhausted horse whose tracks

21

LOUIS L'AMOUR

he had seen had been ridden by either the man who first
greeted him or the girl . . . probably the girl.

Beaupre explained about the Indians Foreman had encountered and the death of his two friends. "I think we've
headed into trouble. The Indians know this place and they'll
need water."

"Best to sit tight, then," Cates advised; "we're safer here
than running."

"My name is Beaupre."

The hesitation was just enough to be noticed. Jennifer
glanced at Logan Cates and he said, looking at her, "I'm Logan
Cates."

Jennifer had heard the name but remembered nothing
about it. Beaupre had smiled a little satisfied smile as if pleased
with himself. Lonnie started to ask a question, then held his
tongue.

"We're going west," Kimbrough said. "The Indians we've
heard of are east of here."

Nobody said anything for several minutes but Cates was
thinking what he knew Beaupre must also think, that there was
no being sure about Indians.

Lonnie phrased it his own way. "I like this place. I'm
staying until we know."

Kimbrough shrugged, then nodded to indicate Lugo. "He's
an Indian . . . what about him?"

"He's a Pima," Beaupre said; "they hate 'Paches more'n
you do."

"He's an Indian. How do we know we can trust him?"

"How do we know we can trust you?" Cates asked mildly.
"Or how can you trust me? We're all strangers here."

Kimbrough's anger showed in his eyes but before he could
speak Jennifer brought the coffee pot to fill Cates's cup. "I trust
him," she said. "My father says the Pimas are good men . . .
the best of men."

Tony Lugo looked up briefly, no expression on his face.
He gave no evidence of being interested in the conversation,
but at her remark he merely glanced briefly at Jennifer. Later,

after Kimbrough had turned impatiently away, Lugo asked Jennifer, "Your hoosband?"

"Not yet . . . not until we get to Yuma Crossing."

It had to be that way, Cates reflected, and Kimbrough was handsome enough to make it understandable, and, judging by his manner, he was a gentleman. Yet there was something about him that did not quite fit, something off-key. It's probably you, he told himself; you're jealous.

He grinned over his cup and Jennifer caught his grin and wondered about it. There was something in Cates's brown, triangular face that was attractive. He was far from handsome, but he was intriguing.

They were good men, Cates was thinking, Beaupre, Lugo, Foreman and Kimbrough . . . every one a fighting man. If they had to make a fight for it the place was right and the company was right. He went to the upper tank and filled his canteens, then went to a shadowed place to lie down. If he had learned one thing from life it was to keep his guns loaded, his canteen full, to eat when there was food and sleep when there was time. A man never knew what would happen; it was best to be ready.

There was a moment before he closed his eyes when he thought of Jennifer Fair. Kimbrough was a fortunate man, a fortunate man, indeed. But Kimbrough had the look of success about him, that easy manner, the polish . . . yet something did not fit, and it was something in the man himself, not the sense of the threadbare about him.

And then he was asleep while the day drew on, the rocks gathered heat, and out upon the desert the heat waves drew a veil across the distance, shimmering like a far-off lake. A fly buzzing around awakened him and Cates slapped it away. It fell on the sand, walked a few uncertain steps, then buzzed off in search of easier game. Cates sat up and mopped the sweat from his face.

Beaupre came down from the rocks after two hours. "A little dust east of here. I figure several men, four to eight, I'd guess."

23

"How far?"

"More'n an hour . . . could be twice that. They are movin' slow, looks like, and this light is deceivin'."

Cates went down into the arroyo to water his horse, and drank beside him. When he got up and drew his hand across his mouth he saw Jennifer watching him. In silence they measured each other, then looked away as if by agreement.

Jennifer felt upset and vaguely resentful. She got up and began to make more coffee. This, at least, she had learned on the ranch, that horse-riding men are always ready for coffee. She watched Cates lead his horse to a shaded place in the arroyo where there was grass. He moved easily . . . somehow he reminded her of a big cat. She decided he was not a mere cowhand, for there was something about him that possessed an assurance, a certainty and boldness that set him apart. She had noticed, too, that Beaupre spoke to him with deference.

Cates . . . it was not a familiar name . . . Logan Cates. The name had a certain rhythm, but she could not remember where she had heard it or if she ever had.

Kimbrough came and sat down beside her. "I wish we could have gone on," he said. "I don't like any of this. I'm sorry I got you into it."

"It's all right."

"Maybe we should try it. In the morning the horses should be ready, and I think we'd have a chance."

"What about the Indians, Grant?"

"They're east of here. They may not even come this far, and I'm sure they wouldn't want to get any nearer the fort than this. Anyway," he added, "the Indian outbreak will stop your father."

"You don't know him."

"Even him," Kimbrough insisted. "It will stop even him."

"Grant, we can't be sure the Indians won't go west. Father has told me of cases where they killed men right outside the walls of a fort. They aren't afraid of the Army, Grant."

Logan Cates came down from the rocks and joined them at

the fireside for coffee. "They're out there," he commented, "but they seem to be waiting for something. Or somebody."

"Who would be out there?" Kimbrough asked impatiently. "Who would be in this infernal desert?"

Cates glanced at him. "A few hours ago," he said, "we were out there."

FOUR

Sergeant Timothy Sheehan called a halt in the bottom of a dry wash, and the men dropped to the sand right in their tracks. Alone, he walked on a few paces and climbed to the lip of the wash and looked across the desert.

Timothy Sheehan had come to the States as a boy of ten and had gone to work at once. At sixteen he joined the Army. At forty-two he was a veteran soldier, leather-hard and leather-tough. Nine years of his service had been at desert outposts and he knew the country well enough to fear it.

An hour earlier they had cut the trail of a small party of Indians headed south, but he was not tracker enough to judge their number accurately. There had been at least six, however, and he was positive they were not of the group who previously attacked them. And this tended to confirm his opinion that something was stirring along the border, and increased his anxiety to report at Yuma.

He lay on the sand, grateful for even this brief respite from the endless plodding. His lips were cracked and his eyes red-rimmed, and he wanted to quit. He wanted to, but knew he could not and would not. He lay there, working out the course they would follow, hating the stale sweaty smell of his

26

unbathed body, of his dusty uniform, and the odor of horse and gunpowder that clung to him.

Including himself there were six men in the group and they had just three horses; until now these had been utilized for transportation of extra rifles, ammunition and canteens. Papago Wells lay at least thirty miles westward of the place where they had been attacked, and despite the long trek already behind them it seemed almost a lifetime away.

Stationed at Fort Yuma only a brief time, he knew little of this country west of Tucson. Water was the first consideration, but Bates Well was dry. Taylor, the last man of the sheriff's posse, told him there was another shallow tank called Cipriano Well . . . uncertain at best. Yet it was their only chance to get water enough to reach Papago Wells.

The low hills on the horizon ahead of him were the Agua Dulces, and Cipriano Well was reported to lie among them. Actually, these so-called wells or tanks were merely catch basins for the runoff from infrequent rains, all highly unreliable. Sheehan knew the water they possessed now was barely sufficient to reach Cipriano, if that tank even existed. There, if there was no water, they must draw lots for three men to take the horses and strike west for Papago.

The sergeant knew the men were near the limit of exhaustion from heat, dehydration and the long march, and he allowed them thirty minutes of rest. At his command they got clumsily to their feet and moved out.

"Keep it closed up," he said; "there's more Indians around."

He let them march for two miles, then halted them. "Conley, Webb and Zimmerman, mount up."

Grinning with cracked lips at the stunned faces of the others, he added, "You'll get your turn. It'll be turn and turn about for the rest of the way."

Taylor hesitated, seemed about to speak, then said nothing. One of the horses was his own and he was subject to no orders, but whatever objection he might have had was stifled by the realization that all were in it together. He was a short, stocky, taciturn man, hardheaded and self-righteous, one of the

27

first to settle at Yuma Crossing after the Army post was established and the ferry resumed.

The sand in the middle of the wash was loose and deep, but that around the edges was mixed with rocks, was firm and made for better walking. It would have been still easier out of the wash but they would have been visible for some distance and Sheehan wanted to invite no trouble.

Dust shifted over their faces and uniforms, but the men plodded on, sodden with weariness, caught up in an almost hypnotic stumbling walk whose very monotony dulled their realization of distance, heat, and dust.

As they walked, Sheehan tried to envisage the situation as it must be, for without doubt Churupati was gathering his forces and a serious outbreak was in prospect. Yet it was unlikely that more than fifty hostiles were in the area, and if they could be pinned down and destroyed the outbreak would be over. His duty was obvious. He must return to Yuma and report to the commanding officer.

Those poor devils caught at isolated ranches or mines were almost sure to be wiped out before help could reach them, if they were not already dead. The few who escaped might make a successful run for it to Yuma or Tucson.

It was sundown when Sheehan's small command reached Cipriano Well.

Taylor had scouted ahead, and as the soldiers drew near he lifted a hand to stop them, then knelt and began to study the tracks. "They've been here, Sergeant, and they have a prisoner."

Sheehan looked at the indicated tracks. Although merged by Indian tracks they were obviously those of a woman . . . a white woman.

Conley had gone on to the well and now he returned. "There's water enough to fill our canteens and water the horses, that's all."

"I'd say five, six Indians." Taylor indicated the stinking carcass of the mule. "Stopped here to butcher the mule and feed up."

Sheehan prowled restlessly. There was nothing they could do about that girl. Without enough horses, without food and more ammunition it would be foolish. "What do you make of this, Taylor?"

For several minutes Taylor studied the tracks indicated by Sheehan, then he said, "Sergeant, that girl got away. She must have waited until they got their bellies full of mule meat and when they dozed off, she walked away."

"Couldn't she take a horse?" Conley asked.

"Afraid she'd spook 'em, I guess. So she just walked off into the desert."

The Indians had followed her. Unless she was crazy with luck they would have recaptured her by now. Sheehan searched the desert, using his glass, but the shimmering heat waves cut him off from the distance and the desert told him nothing. Whatever had happened must have been hours ago.

"Last night, some time," Taylor said. "She couldn't have gone far before they caught up."

"Maybe." Sheehan studied the tracks. "She was moving right out, Taylor. Smart, too. Notice she didn't try to run? She knew it would kill her off too soon . . . I'd say she has a chance." He looked up. "All right, men. When the canteens are full, we move out."

"Sarge," Conley suggested, "how's about two, three of us pushin' on a-horseback? We might come up in time to save that girl."

"No. We stick together."

Sweat trickled down his face and neck. How far could a young girl walk in a night? He watched his small column form up, and then he moved them out. If that girl had only had sense enough to hole up somewhere and wait them out, she might still be safe. It was a mighty small chance, yet a chance.

He started west, walking toward the setting sun. It would soon be dark and the men were all in, or they should have been, yet for the first time since the march began they moved out as if eager to be going. Even big Zimmerman, sullen and hard-eyed, seemed anxious to be moving.

29

Twice during the long night he halted his men and allowed them an hour of sleep, and then moved them out again. There was little more that human strength could endure, but he had his command to consider as well as the girl. Despite the additional water they now had, he knew the sun took as much strength from his men as did the walking, and they needed distance behind them. Despite the brutal pace, nobody complained. Everyone understood that he was leading them in a struggle for survival.

The sky was faintly gray but the sun had not yet risen when the first break came in their chain of bad luck. Emerging from a nest of scattered boulders they saw, not many yards away, an Indian on a paint pony. He was sitting absolutely motionless, all his attention on something in the rocks ahead of them. At Sheehan's up-thrown hand, the men stopped.

Whatever it was the Indian watched was further ahead in the same jumble of gigantic boulders, and as they watched another Indian appeared, stalking something they could not see.

Sheehan gestured for Conley, Webb and Zimmerman to move toward the outer edge of the field of rocks, a point from which they would have outflanked the Indian on the pony. The rest he waved into position near him.

He waited. If the Indians found the girl first it would complicate matters, for if attacked she would be instantly killed. Nevertheless he wanted at least two Indians in plain sight before—

"*Fire!*"

The crashing volley cut short his command, and the Indian on the horse jerked from the impact of bullets and tumbled to the ground. Higher on the slope the second Indian took two running steps, then pitched headlong into the sand, sliding a little way and smearing blood.

Conley, on the extreme right, fired suddenly, then fired again.

Sheehan hated to expose his men but there was the girl to consider. "As skirmishers!" he yelled. "Yo-ho-o-o!"

They moved out on the double. There was a shot from the rocks that missed, and then the soldiers were weaving among the rocks. Zimmerman moved in, clubbed his rifle, and Styles fired. From beyond the rocks there was a rush of hoofs and then silence.

The soldiers moved on through the rocks. Three Indians were riding away, one swaying in the saddle, obviously in bad shape. Three Indians lay dead, and Sergeant Sheehan felt grim satisfaction at getting a little of their own back.

Among the rocks, from a crevice that seemed too narrow to hold even a child, the girl stood up. She was very thin and her flimsy dress blew in the wind, flapping around her childish figure.

"I'm Junie Hatchett," she said, "and I'm most awful glad to see you!"

FIVE

Logan Cates was again on lookout when he saw distant dust against the blue morning, but knowing how many illusions the desert offered, he waited. There had been, a little earlier, a faint sound of rifle fire in the east, but he might have been mistaken.

Undoubtedly the marchers he saw had been on the trail all night to have arrived at this place at such an hour. This made it doubtful they were Indians.

It was still cool . . . a quail called out, somewhere to the south among the lava boulders, and he was sure this was a real quail. There had been some the night before about which he had many doubts. That lava field stretched all the way to the Gulf of California. What had Cortez called it? The Vermilion Sea? Or was it someone before Cortez?

His eyes continued their restless search of the lava and the sand dunes. Without doubt they were observed, but from where?

The approaching dust hung almost still in the desert air. Not all the group could be horsemen, they moved too slowly for this. Was there a hint of blue in the dust? Logan Cates studied it through the glasses but could not be sure.

A boot scraped on the rock behind him and he recognized

the shadow as that of Jennifer Fair. She was shading her eyes toward the dust column, and he got to his feet, his rifle in the hollow of his arm. "I think it's the Army," he said, "and in bad shape."

"There's a girl with them."

He knew it was none of his business but something impelled him to ask, "Are you really going to marry him?"

Her eyes when she turned to look at him were level and cool. "I believe that is my business, Mr. Cates."

"Of course."

"He's a gentleman," she added, and was immediately angry for defending him. "He has breeding."

"So has his horse . . . but I wouldn't pick him to ride in this country."

"I don't intend to live in this country."

"Then you should do all right." Her comment rankled, and he said irritably, "What's wrong with this country? Your father likes it. He helped to open it up."

"I've seen how a country like this is opened up and I don't like it. I doubt, Mr. Cates, if you could understand how I feel." She looked directly into his eyes. "I know the kind of man you are."

"Do you?" He narrowed his eyes as they swept the lava and sand. "I don't believe it. I don't believe you know anything about a man like me or a country like this. It takes rough men, Miss Fair, to tame a rough country; rough men, but good men. Your father is in that class. As for you, I don't think you'd measure up, and you'll do well to leave it. You're a hothouse flower, very soft, very appealing and very useless."

"You aren't very complimentary."

"Should I be?" He glanced at the end of his cigarette, then his eye caught a flicker of movement and he held himself very still, keyed for action until he saw it was a tiny lizard, struggling with some insect at the edge of a bush. "In the world you are going to, men want pretty, useless women. They want toys for their lighter moments, and we have those women out here,

33

too, only we have another name for them. We want women here who can make a home, and if need be, handle a rifle."

"And you don't think I could?"

"You're quitting, aren't you? You're running away?"

"My father can get along without me. He has done so for years."

"And probably during all those years he has been looking forward to the day when you would be with him. What do you suppose a man like your father works for? He worked for you, for your children . . . if you ever have any."

He was angry and he knew he was saying things he should not say, that were none of his business. "And what about him?" He jerked his thumb toward where Kimbrough lay sleeping. "He's running, isn't he? Why didn't he stay and face your father? Why didn't he stay there and tell your father he was going to marry you and if he didn't like it, he knew what he could do."

"You don't know my father."

Cates grinned, suddenly amused that she should cause him to become so angry. "I know his type, and it would take more than Kimbrough has to face him. You know what I think, ma'am? You feel the same way."

She was stiff with anger. She wanted to walk away but did not want him to believe her defeated. She desperately wanted the last word and could not find it. The soldiers were near enough now so their faces could be seen, and one of them stumbled and fell, pulling himself up with an effort.

"Why don't you go down there and help them, if you are so self-sufficient? Why don't you do something?"

"My grandfather went out to meet some men in uniform once, ma'am, and they turned out to be Indians in uniforms they'd taken from dead soldiers. I'll wait until I can see the whites of their hides."

He dropped his cigarette to the lava rock and carefully rubbed it out with the toe of his boot. She had often seen her father do the same thing in the same, identical way, and it angered her.

34

Cates laid the barrel of his Winchester across the top of a boulder. "All right." He did not seem to speak loudly yet the ragged little column swayed to a halt. "Hold up, down there! Who are you?"

The dust settled around them. The square-built man stepped forward. "Sergeant Sheehan, United States Cavalry, four soldiers and two civilians. Who are you?"

"Come on in, Sergeant! And welcome to the family!"

Foreman, Beaupre and Kimbrough were on their feet, watching the soldiers come in. With a shade of impatience she noticed that Grant was the last to leave his blanket and it infuriated her that Cates noticed it also. She glared at him but he merely grinned and looked away.

Logan Cates remained where he was, hearing the excited conversation as they compared notes with the soldiers. He did not need to talk to them to understand what must have happened; their appearance spoke for itself. So much time was wasted in idle chatter, and he knew this was a dangerous time, when Indians might attack, knowing the excitement of the new arrivals would distract the defending forces. Nothing of the kind happened, however, and he sat watching the desert, remembering other times like this, and thinking of Jim Fair.

He knew the rancher by reputation only, but he had a name for being a hard man as well as a good one. He could understand such a man, for he had an idea that Jim Fair was much like himself. There is nothing easy about building a cattle outfit in a wild, barren country, nothing easy about fighting Apaches and outlaws, and it can be a hard, lonely life, far from the refining aspects of feminine society. The home a man would want, the comfort, the ease, the little things, the nice things, these a man alone on the desert could not have, and it took a woman to bring them to him. What he had told Jennifer Fair was, he believed, the truth. Jim Fair had undoubtedly longed for the return of his daughter, for the home she could make for him, and for the pleasure of seeing her marry and rear children. Cates had seen too many of those bluff, hard old frontiersmen not to know the breed.

Lonnie came up to relieve him and he went down and walked right into trouble.

Jim Beaupre was standing off to one side, his big hands hanging at his sides. He looked then just what he was, a hard old man. Taylor faced him.

"If that's how you want it," Taylor was saying, and he would have reached for his gun.

"Stop it!" Cates's voice rang with command. "Don't you damn fools realize we've trouble enough!"

"This man's wanted in Yuma!" Taylor replied stubbornly. "He was one of them we were chasin' when we ran into the Indians."

"Save your shells," Cates advised. "You'll be glad of each other before we get out of this."

"Are you taking up for this outlaw?"

"When we're out of this if you two still want to kill each other, just have at it. Now you'll listen to me."

"And who the hell are you?"

"Mr. Taylor," Sheehan interposed, "I'd listen to this man if I were you. We can't have any trouble here. Not now."

Taylor was not convinced. A stubborn man, he had been sworn in as a deputy and the fact that he alone survived meant little to him. He had started to do a job and he intended to finish it. "I'm in the right," he insisted; "this man Beaupre is wanted by the law."

"Bein' right can get you killed," Beaupre said.

Logan Cates shot him a glance. "Shut up!" he said harshly. "And Taylor, why don't you go get some coffee?"

Taylor's face was flushed and angry, but he turned abruptly away and walked to the fire.

Jim Beaupre stared after him, then bit off a corner of his plug of tobacco. "Thanks, Logan. If those folks at Yuma would keep their trouble-happy kids in line there'd have been no trouble. They jumped Lugo an' me because we were strangers an' fair game."

"Your problem," Cates replied shortly. "Only as long as we're in trouble here, try to keep shy of him."

36

He crossed to the rocks and sat down with his back to them, knowing this was only the beginning. Once the fighting started all would be well, but until then they could expect only trouble.

Sheehan squatted on his heels. "Hotheaded fools. I'm glad you stopped that."

"The first thing we've got to watch," Cates said, thinking ahead, "is our horses. They'll try to stampede 'em if they can, and set us afoot, so what we've got to do is build a corral. If we lose those horses we'll never get to Yuma, Indians or no Indians."

Sheehan nodded wearily. "You're right, but my men are all in, dead beat."

Cates got up and spoke loudly enough for them all to hear. "We've got to build a corral to hold the horses. Any volunteers?"

Jim Beaupre was the first man on his feet, and Taylor, determined not to let Beaupre out of his sight, also got up. Kimbrough, Conley and Zimmerman followed. Cates led the way into the arroyo and finding a thick wall of brush, he started breaking off wands of ocotillo to thread into the brush. Tying branches of the brush together, weaving the spiked wands of ocotillo and other branches into the brush, they soon had woven a tight fence against stampede. Seeing what he was doing the others had caught on quickly, Lugo among them.

It was very hot in the deep arroyo. They worked steadily and their combined efforts soon had created a solid wall of brush that not even a bull could crash through. Where there were gaps in the defenses around the edges of the arroyo they filled in with stones.

When they had finished their work, Sheehan dropped to the sand beside Cates. The heat was stifling. "You Army?" Sheehan asked.

"Once, briefly."

"Somebody's got to be in command."

"Kimbrough was a Confederate colonel, I think." Cates was noncommittal.

"We need an Indian fighter." Sheehan looked down at his

37

hands. "I seem to recall a Cates who was chief of scouts with Crook."

"It was for a short time only."

"Good enough for me. Crook knew Indian fighters better than any of them. If you were good enough to scout for him, that's all I need to know."

"It was just a campaign along the border and into Mexico."

"Crook was the best of them all." Sheehan got up. "Maybe we should put it to a vote."

Sheehan proposed it. They needed one man to lead, a man who knew Indians, a man who could command. He suggested Logan Cates.

"Grant Kimbrough," Jennifer said. "I believe he would be the man. He was a colonel in the Confederate Army."

"Cates is good enough for me," Beaupre said.

Taylor's head came up sharply. "Kimbrough," he said.

Conley was half asleep, but he opened his eyes and let them go from one man to the other. "Cates," he said, and closed his eyes again.

Zimmerman voted for Kimbrough, but Junie nodded to indicate Cates. "Him," she said. "I think he'd do fine."

Styles indicated Kimbrough. "I'll stick with the Army," he said, "Union or Johnny Reb."

Kimbrough glanced at Cates, smiling a little. "Well?"

Sheehan got up and dusted the sand off his breeches. "Nobody has asked the kid up there." He turned and looked up at the rocks. "Hey, up there! We're votin' for a commanding officer! It's Kimbrough or Cates. Which do you say?"

Lonnie Foreman never took his eyes from the desert. "Cates," he said.

Kimbrough shrugged. "Looks like a draw," he said.

Beaupre jerked his head to indicate Lugo, who had not spoken. "What about him? He ain't voted yet."

"The Injun?" Taylor was startled. "When could an Injun vote?"

"If he can shoot," Sheehan said, "he can vote."

"That's fine with me," Kimbrough said. "What do you say, Lugo?"

Tony Lugo was digging in the sand with his fingers. He glanced up, his black eyes, like flakes of obsidian, revealing nothing. "Him." He indicated Cates. "I think he know Indian."

Grant Kimbrough glanced at Cates, his face unreadable, then he shrugged. "All right, Captain," he said, "what are your orders?"

"Two men with the horses at all times. Nobody outside the circle of defense without orders, the lookout to be relieved every two hours, all rifles checked at once, two at a time." He turned to Sheehan. "Sergeant, check the ammunition and food. I want an actual count, no guesses."

"Yes, sir."

Beaupre climbed the rocks to relieve Foreman, and when Lonnie came down, Cates intercepted him. "If you get a chance," he said softly, "talk to that girl. She's lonesome and scared."

"I'm not much hand—not talking to women."

"She'll listen to you." Cates hesitated. "She's a kid, Lonnie, and she's trying to play the woman. She's trying very hard, so help her out. Just talk to her . . . it doesn't matter what about, help her loosen up, help her get rid of that fear. She's been scared, kid, and those Indians are still out there. Just don't talk about her or about Indians."

"I never talked to no girl. I wouldn't know what to say."

"You'll think of something. She's scared, Lonnie, and tied up tight as a fiddle string inside. You . . . you're closer to her age, like boys she'd meet at a dance or somewhere. You've got to help her."

"Well . . . all right."

Cates climbed the rocks and looked over the desert, refusing Beaupre's offer of a chew of tobacco. "Thanks," Beaupre said, "for pullin' Taylor off me. That was a fair shootin' back yonder."

"Stay away from him."

"Taylor's one of those sanctimonious blisters who believes

39

LOUIS L'AMOUR

any accused man is guilty. Hell, I don't want to kill him, but
he's got it in his craw and his kind won't quit."

"It'll work out."

Logan Cates was far from sure. Taylor was a tenacious man
sure of his own rightness, and not one to back away from
trouble. It was this quality in him that could get him killed.

Restlessly, Cates scouted the small perimeter of their position. The three pools lay in the arroyo which fell away grad-
ually from the upper to the lower. The difference in the levels
of the first two was slight, the third greater, and from there the
arroyo widened to almost a hundred feet. Below it was still
wider, much of it choked with brush, while the edges of the
arroyo were also a dense thicket. The lookout place chosen was
just above the higher and smaller of the tanks. There, among
the lava boulders, was a good observation point and an excellent firing position. Lower down the arroyo was the freshly
made wall of ocotillo branches and woven brush to corral the
horses. The position occupied was extensive, but easily defended, for it was accessible from the outside at few points, and
without worming through dense brush it was impossible to see
into the corral where the horses were kept. Yet there was
much cover for an attacking force as well, cover such as Indians
knew well how to use.

Nevertheless, the situation could scarcely be improved.
They had water, enough to last for weeks, they had some food,
they had ammunition, and they had some good fighting men.

It was almost dusk before Lonnie managed to get close
enough to Junie Hatchett to talk. She was drying her hair,
which she had washed in water scooped into a rock hollow
which served as a basin.

"Sure is good to have a woman around," Lonnie suggested
tentatively. "Miss Jennifer likes it, too, I reckon, her being
alone with us before."

Junie said nothing, keeping busy with her hair, not even
glancing his way. He watched the shadows on the darkening
water.

40

"Mighty pretty here," he said, "an' quiet, too."

She was using the pool for a mirror, but her face was only dimly visible now and soon it would be too dark to see.

"I figure California to be a comin' country," he said. "A man could make a start. Maybe get himself a piece of land."

She sat back on her heels, but did not look at him. Cates, some distance off, was sure she was listening.

"Ain't like I had anybody to go back to," Lonnie said. "I can stay out here easy as not. I like to have me a few cows and some fruit trees. A little place. Somewhere with good water, and a house I build myself. I helped build two, three houses an' I figure I can build me a good one."

Junie looked at herself in the water, but even the dim outline was losing itself in the dark. She felt she was like that, lost in the dark somewhere, and no way out. Only there was a single bright star in the sky over the edge of the lava cliff, and Lonnie Foreman was talking to her.

"Maybe I could find a place near the mountains, somewhere with trees and grass. I like to have a place like that." He paused, looking at the star's bright lantern over the rocks. "Kind of a lot to do . . . a man alone like that."

He was silent for several minutes. "You know what I miss out here? I miss jelly an' jam. Back to home we always had it. Ma, she put it up an' when fall come there it was, all in jars in the cellar catching dust, but just waitin' to be et up. I used to like to go down there when I was little, just to see the light from the lantern on those dusty jars full of peaches and cherries and the like. Don't expect I'll ever see jelly like that again. Or jam."

Junie fingered her drying hair and tried to straighten her dress.

"I like it with hot biscuits," he said. "Just thinkin' of it makes me hungry."

Logan Cates looked out over the desert, feeling the coolness, remembering hot biscuits he had known as a boy, and remembering so much else along with it. A man lost a lot, growing up, a lot he could never regain. He shook his head, melancholy, and filled suddenly with a nameless longing.

"I never could talk to girls," Lonnie sounded his defeat. "I never know what to say."

"You talk all right," Junie said.

SIX

When he heard the quail call he knew their time of waiting would soon be past, for this was no true quail. He could not have told how he knew, it was one of those things a man learned, something he absorbed as he lived in wild country. It was like finding a lost trail in the dark, or one of those prehistoric Indian trails you could not quite see but you knew was a trail just the same.

He also knew they were free of attack during the night—probably.

It was a superstition of many Indian tribes that a warrior slain in the dark must forever wander, lost in the stygian darkness of the space between the worlds of the living and the dead. Their respite would end with the dawn.

But a watch would be kept anyway. There might be skeptics among these Indians, skeptics who ignored the old superstitions. More than once he had been laughed at for being too careful, and had helped to bury some of the men who were not careful.

With the first red arrows of the sun the attack would come out of the desert, for he had seen the dust in the sunset and knew there were more Indians now. He had seen the dust trails against the far blue mountains, hanging like smoke against the distance. The Indians would come out with the new day, their dusty brown bodies seeming to spring from the sand itself, and they would vanish as suddenly. Men had died by the dozen in the desert who had never known an Indian was near; he had himself seen a soldier killed by an Indian the soldier had passed within twenty yards in broad daylight on the open desert.

Uneasy with inaction he went to his gear and shifted from boots to moccasins. Sheehan watched him curiously, and Cates told him, "I'm going to scout around out there."

"You're takin' a chance."

"I get around pretty good."

He went over the rocks and eased himself down at the edge of the ironwood thicket. He took his time, knowing haste could be dangerous, and he settled down in the brush and listened. After a long time he moved, gliding on silent feet among the rocks, making no smallest whisper of sound. Several times he paused to listen, checking all the night sounds.

The rustle of leaves, the scurry of a small animal or lizard, the rattle of a pebble loosened by erosion . . . these were different sounds than the movement of a man.

When he came out of the desert Jennifer was momentarily frightened. Grant had returned to their saddles for his pipe, and she was alone. To the south the twin peaks of Pinacate were dimly visible against the night sky.

"You frightened me."

Cates stopped beside her, looking at the desert and the night. It was very still; the vast country to the south looked like hell with the fires out. "So peaceful," he said, "and so dangerous."

"Are there Indians out there? Really, I mean?"

"There are."

"But it's so quiet!"

"That's proof enough. The desert has its own small sounds and when you don't hear them something is out there warning them to be still."

"If there are Indians, why did you go out?"

"Looking at the places they'll use for cover when they attack."

"You might have been killed. You were inviting trouble."

"Yes, I might have been killed. Each of us is in deadly danger every instant from now until we get to Yuma. But I wasn't looking for trouble—only a fool takes chances. Fools or children who don't know any better. Danger is never pretty, it's never thrilling. It's dirty, bloody and miserable. It's choking dust, the pain of wounds and waiting that eats your guts out.

"Nobody but a fool or some crazy kid goes hunting trouble. It's different when you meet it face to face on a dark night than when you read of it in a book. All this talk of people who look for adventure is from people who've had no experience."

He dropped his cigarette. "Your father knows. He lived through it, trying to make this country safe for you to grow up in."

"You don't approve of me, do you?"

"What is there to approve of? You are beautiful, of course, yet you resent the very things that made life easy for you. You resent your father. From the summit of the molehill of your Eastern education you judge the mountain of the obstacles your father faced. You—" he turned away from her "—are like the froth on beer. You look nice but you don't mean anything."

He walked to the fire, angry with himself for saying things he had no right to say, for venturing opinions that were none of his business. He did not know Jim Fair, but he knew a little of any man who came to a country like this when Jim Fair came, who stayed and who built something from nothing. It took strength, character, and a kind of dogged determination that was wholly admirable. It also took fighting ability, and above all judgment.

He crouched by the fire and ate the slice of beef Junie Hatchett brought to him between two thick slices of bread. He ate hungrily, careful not to look into the fire. Staring into fires was reserved for tenderfeet or more civilized worlds. A man who looks into a fire sees nothing when he turns quickly to look into the dark, and his momentary blindness may cost his life.

Grant Kimbrough came down from the rocks with Jennifer. She looked angry, and Logan Cates grinned wryly, knowing that it was himself at whom she was angry.

"Find any Indians?" Kimbrough asked, and there was an edge of sarcasm in his tone.

"I wasn't looking for any."

Sergeant Sheehan joined them at the fire, and the light from the flames caught the scattered silver in his hair. "How many d' you figure, Cates?"

"Anywhere from twenty to twice that number. Not more than fifty."

"How can you estimate?" Kimbrough asked.

" 'Paches never travel in big bunches. They live off the desert and there's never food or water enough for a big bunch. Nine out of ten war parties will number from ten to thirty warriors. Churupati could never get more than sixty, and my guess is there are not over twenty or twenty-five out there."

Zimmerman stood by the fire listening. He was a huge, hairy man who badly needed a shave. His mood seemed surly, and he looked up at Cates with a challenge. "You sure about that Indian?"

"Lugo? He's a Pima."

Zimmerman threw the remains of his coffee on the sand with a violent gesture. "So he's a Pima," he said angrily. "I heard you say that before. I say he's an Indian and they're all alike. He should be tied up."

"He won't be," Logan Cates spoke mildly. "He's one of our best men."

"You say. I say the way to begin this fight is to shoot that greasy mongrel."

"Anybody," Cates spoke mildly still, "who lifts a hand against that Indian will answer to me."

Zimmerman hesitated, his face ugly. For a moment it was obvious that he wanted to challenge this statement. Sergeant Sheehan interrupted.

"That's enough of that, Zimmerman. We're all under the command of Cates. You'll obey orders."

"You mean you'd have me court-martialed?" Zimmerman sneered. "Don't take me for a fool! When all this is over there won't be enough of us left to tell the story. You won't carry any tales, nor will anybody else."

Zimmerman walked away into the darkness and Sheehan looked after him in silence.

Beaupre came to the edge of the rocks above. "Cates, there's shootin' off to the east—mighty far off."

He climbed the rocks again, glad to escape the situation at the fire. They listened, but there was no further sound. He seated himself among the rocks near Beaupre and waited for a repetition of the sound, but they heard nothing. Irritably, he considered the situation below. Zimmerman was a dangerous man, unwilling to accept authority, and his remarks to Sheehan, uttered in the tone used, were practically a threat. As if there was not trouble enough with the Indians, there had to be trouble within their own circle.

Despite the fact that he had been pursued by a sheriff's posse, Jim Beaupre was a good man, a solid man, definitely a man to have on your side in any kind of a fight. Cates knew his kind from other times and places, for Beaupre was the sort of man who was handy at any job or with any weapon, and he was the sort who would, when the frontier ended, settle down to one of his jobs without fuss or strain. He would be a teamster, a blacksmith, a small rancher, never wealthy but always hard-working.

And what of you, Logan Cates? he asked himself. Where will you be, and what will you become?

Some day he would be too slow with his gun, would break a leg somewhere in the desert or lose his canteen too far from water. It had happened to others, it could happen to him. He would never have the ranch he wanted with a stream of running water and some old oak trees, he would never have the time to do the reading he wanted. His father had been a great one to read; he had been reading the night Dave Horne shot him through the window.

Only Dave Horne had reckoned without Logan, who was sixteen at the time, but fully aged in the six-shooter. Logan dropped Horne with a bullet through the skull before he got out of the yard.

"That shootin' bothers me." Beaupre interrupted his thinking. "Somebody's in trouble out there."

There was nothing anyone could do, so they sat tight, waiting for further shooting, or some evidence of movement. Kimbrough came up into the rocks, and Lonnie Foreman followed.

Several minutes passed, and then suddenly, far off in the night, but rapidly coming nearer, they heard the sound of running hoofs . . . somebody was hunting a hole, and coming fast.

There was a shot, closer than they had expected, for they all saw the stab of flame in the night, and then other shots.

The horse came with a rush, leaping over the rocks, a led horse following. The horse came like the black rush of doom, nostrils distended. The horse skidded to a halt in their midst and a woman slid to the ground, a heavy old-style Remington pistol in her hand.

She was a fat, heavy woman with a wide face and a smile to fit, and she glanced around swiftly as she touched the ground. Despite her escape there was neither fear nor relief in her eyes, just a swift calculation of the situation. When she spoke, which was immediately, her voice was hoarse, hard and cheerful. "Well, slap me with a silver dollar if this isn't something like it! Ten minutes ago I'd have sold my hide for a phony peso!"

She glanced around again. "Boys, I'm Big Maria out of Kansas City by way of Wichita, Abilene and El Paso, and am I glad to see you! Has anybody got a drink?"

SEVEN

Startled, they could merely stare, but the fat woman was not disturbed. She smiled broadly and winked at Beaupre. "Never was so glad to see anybody in my life! Pete, he tol' me about this here waterhole. Said if anything happened to him to run for it."

Logan Cates remained in the background, looking past her at the powerful horse with its bulging saddlebags. It was a magnificent animal and in splendid shape. His eyes strayed to the fetlocks and then returned to Big Maria.

"We figured ever'body from here to Tucson was either holed up or dead."

"We come right out of Tucson! Pete, he caught himself a slug in a shindig there, so we hightailed it." She smiled broadly. "He wasn't so much worried about the slug he caught as the five he put into the other gent!

"Well, he should have set still, because we run head-on into a passel of Indians. Pete, he opened up with a shotgun at bellyshootin' range and got himself a couple before they nailed him. I grabbed his Winchester and lit a shuck."

Jennifer had come from the curtained-off space under the overhang. "You must be Jim Fair's daughter," Big Maria said.

"You know my father?"

49

"No, but I saw him an' heard him! He's madder than a rattlesnake with a tied tail! Said a no-account tinhorn ran off with his daughter!" She grinned widely at the circle of listeners. "Which one of you no-account tinhorns is the lucky man?"

Grant Kimbrough's face flushed to the roots of his hair. "Miss Fair and I are going to be married," he said stiffly.

Big Maria chuckled. "Mister, you an' her are goin' to be married if Big Jim don't catch you! If he does he'll brand you with a number-ten boot!"

Jennifer turned sharply away, her face white with humiliation. Grant Kimbrough hesitated as if about to reply, then turned and hurried after her.

Logan Cates walked back to his place among the rocks and Beaupre descended to lead the horses away, but not until Big Maria had deftly retrieved the saddlebags. Those horses were in fine shape, much better shape than any horse he'd ever seen that came over the trail that lay behind them.

The time was short now. There was faint yellow over the eastern mountains.

Mile after mile the gray sands stretched away into the vague pre-dawn light, here and there a bit of white where lay the bleaching skeletons of horses who had died on this road, known for many years as Camino del Diablo, or the Devil's Highway. During the few years when the road was followed during the gold rush more than four hundred people had died of thirst, and the vague line through the sand hills and ridges of naked rock was marked by whitening bones and the occasional wrecks of abandoned wagons. On his first trip over the road he had counted more than sixty graves in a day's travel, and nobody knew how many had died whose bones lay scattered by coyotes and unburied.

No command was needed as the morning grew lighter. One by one the defenders slipped into position and lay waiting, listening to the morning sounds and waiting, knowing whatever was to happen would begin today.

Or would it?

Logan Cates remembered the stories of Churupati. The

50

man was cunning as a wolf, shrewd, dangerous, and untiring. Nor was he a man liable to risk his few followers unless the gain was sure to be great. Here within the oval among the lava rocks defended by the few white men were horses, guns, and ammunition, all of which he could use. Above all, the chances of relief were small, so if he could find water, he had only to wait. Churupati knew what hunger could do, what waiting could do, and what the straining of nerves could do.

The shot came suddenly out of an empty desert, struck a rock within inches of Lonnie's head, and ricocheted with an angry whine.

From behind them, over in the lava rocks, another shot was fired.

After that, there was silence. Silence, solitude, and the rising sun. With the rising sun the coolness was gone. An hour passed, and then another. Suddenly, from near the horses, there was a sudden burst of firing followed by a single shot, then a pair of shots. Kimbrough, Lugo and Beaupre were down there.

Sheehan crawled up to join Cates. "Killed a horse," he said sourly.

Cates glanced at him sharply, worried about the dun. "No," Sheehan said, "it wasn't yours—it was mine."

"One less. I hope you're a good walker, Sergeant."

"I'd walk or crawl." Sheehan wiped the sweatband of his hat. "I'd do either willingly to get out alive."

Silence held the desert, and the sky was without clouds. Only the heat waves shimmered. Sheehan shifted his rifle in his hands and wiped his sweaty palms on his shirt front.

"Cates," he spoke in a low tone, "don't count on help from the fort. Not soon, anyway. With us gone there aren't twenty men there."

Lonnie Foreman turned impatiently. "Why are they waiting? If they're going to attack, why don't they get started?"

"Who knows why an Indian does anything? Maybe they figure they don't have to hurry."

51

Lonnie was silent and when he spoke he said, "You know what I think? I think maybe they're right."

From Kimbrough's position there was a single shot, then silence, and no sound but the light breeze of a gray morning turning to a blazing hot day.

Sheehan slipped away to scout the various positions and check with his men. Lonnie shifted his rifle and squinted his eyes against the sun. "She's a real nice girl," he said suddenly.

Cates agreed solemnly. "Make some man a good wife," he added.

"If I was a little older," Lonnie explained carefully, "I'd—no, I want to see some more country. Why, I hear tell that up north in California there's some of the biggest trees in the world! I'd sure like to see them trees."

"You do that." Cates had found a cluster of rocks in the sand that somehow did not look quite natural. "I figure every man should see some trees before he dies."

He lifted his Winchester and sighted at the flat surface of a rock slightly behind the group. He steadied himself, blinked the sweat from his eyes, then squeezed off his shot.

From behind the rocks there was a startled yelp and Cates fired against the rock again, then fired past the rock. There was no further sound.

"Them ricochets," Lonnie said, "they tear a man up. They tear him up something fierce."

Cates slid back to where it was safe, then stood up. "You stay here, Lonnie. They'll be nervous now, but you be careful." He started down the rocks. "She's a fine girl, all right. I'd say she was very fine."

He stopped by the fire for coffee. He squatted by the fire, thinking about it. The killing of that horse had been no accident, for every horse killed meant a man afoot, and a man walking was a man who would die in this country.

Zimmerman walked to the fire and lifted the coffee pot. Cates saw at a glance that the big man was hunting trouble, and it would be always that way with Zimmerman. He would hunt trouble until somebody killed him—only this was not the time.

"You wet-nursin' that Injun?" Zimmerman demanded.

"Before we get out of here we'll be glad to have him with us. We'll need every man we've got."

"Send him out there with the rest of the Injuns," Zimmerman said. "He's like them all. This here's a place for white men."

"Lugo is a Pima, and the Pimas are good Indians. They are ancient enemies of both the Apaches and the Yaqui, with more reason for hating them than you'll ever have. He stays."

"Maybe." Zimmerman gulped coffee, then wiped his mouth with the back of his hand. "Maybe I'll run him out."

"In the first place"—Logan Cates got to his feet—"Tony Lugo is, I suspect, twice the fighter you've ever been. In the second place, I'm in command here, and if you want to start anything with him, start it with me first."

Zimmerman looked at him over the coffee pot, a slow, measuring glance, and he did not like what he saw. He had seen these lean, quiet men before, and there was a cool certainty in Cates's manner that betrayed the fact that he was no stranger to trouble. Yet Zimmerman knew his own enormous strength and relied upon it. "You get in my way," he said, "and I'll take that little gun and put it where it belongs."

"How about right now?" Cates asked softly.

Zimmerman looked at him, then shook his head. "I'll pick my own time," he said, "but you stay out of my way."

Turning, the big soldier walked away, and Logan Cates knew that only the time was suspended, that nothing had been avoided. Nor could there be any reasoning with Zimmerman, for the man's hatred of all Indians had been absorbed during childhood, drilled into him, leaving no room for reason; for such a man the loss of an arm would come easier than the loss of prejudice, for he lived by hatred.

The attack came suddenly. The Apaches came out of the desert like brown ghosts, and vanished as suddenly. They had come with a rush, moving suddenly as on signal, but there had

53

been no signal that anyone heard. They came, they fired and they hit the sand, and then the desert was empty again, as though the sudden movement had been a deception of the sunlight on the sand . . . only now they were closer.

Another horse had been killed, and Cates swore under his breath, knowing what the Indians had in mind.

For a time there was silence and every man waited, expecting another rush, searching the sand and the jumble of lava for a target they really did not expect to find. Sheehan mopped sweat from his brow and worried, wondering what had been done back at the fort, knowing how few men were there.

"Nobody to shoot at," Foreman complained. "They're like ghosts."

"We wasted time!" Taylor said irritably. "We could have struck out for Yuma."

"Like your posse did?" Cates asked.

"That was an accident!" Taylor said angrily. "It wouldn't happen again."

"The Apaches make accidents like that."

Beaupre and Lugo fired as one man, and Kimbrough's shot was an instant behind. The three bullets furrowed the crest of a sand hill a short distance off, a crest where an instant before an Indian had showed.

"Missed him!" Beaupre spat his disgust.

"Teach 'em to be careful," Lonnie Foreman assured him. "If you missed you sure made him unhappy, comin' that near."

Minutes paced slowly by. Out over the desert heat waves shimmered; the day was going now, and it would leave them in darkness soon, leave them in darkness where the Apaches could creep closer, and closer.

Cates moved around their position, checking each man, scanning the desert from every vantage point. The area they covered was all of a hundred yards long, but difficult to get at for any attacker. There was cover beyond their perimeter of defense, but the cover for the defenders was even better. Where the two upper pools were there was a wide space that was open and safe as long as the defenders could keep the Indians out of the bordering rocks.

The hours drew slowly on. Occasionally a shot came out of the desert . . . or an arrow. But there were no more casualties. Only once did anyone get a shot, and it was Kimbrough. He took a shot at a running Indian, a shadow seen among the mesquite and cholla, no more. Whether he scored or missed there was no way of telling. The sun lowered itself slowly behind the distant hills, and out over the lava, a quail called. It was evening again.

Squatting beside the fire, Cates nursed his cup in his hands. The fire and the coffee were the only friendly things; he did not belong here, he did not want this fight. Alone, he might have gone on, for his horse was a desert horse and his two canteens were large. And now he was pinned here, surrounded by Indians, and among people either indifferent to him or outright in their dislike of him.

"Will we get out?" Jennifer asked him.

"We'll get out."

"Do you suppose—I mean, is this all? Or are there other Indians out?"

"Can't say."

"I was wondering because of my father. I—I think he's looking for me."

"I would be, if I was him."

"Why? I love Grant. I intend to marry him."

"All right."

"You don't like him, do you?"

Cates shrugged. "I don't know him. He may be a good man . . . but not for you."

"You don't think much of me, either."

"You'll do all right as soon as you understand what your dad means to this country, and what the country means to him."

"He killed a man. I saw him."

"Before we get out of here," Cates replied, "we'll all have killed men. Or we'll have been killed ourselves."

55

"That's different!"

"Is it?" Cates indicated Kimbrough. "What about him? He was in the war, so what about the killing he did?"

"But that was war!"

"Your dad was in a war, too, only it was fought without banners, without the big battalions. It was fought by a few men, or fought alone and without help . . . it was a war to survive, and they survived; they built the country. Every meal you've eaten, every gown you've worn, every bit of it was bought with the results of that war."

"I saw my father kill a boy . . . just a boy!"

"Uh-huh . . . but that boy carried a man's gun, didn't he?"

Cates got up. "This is a rough country, ma'am. It needs men with the bark on . . . and it needs women, women who could rear strong sons." He indicated Junie Hatchett. "There's a girl to ride the river with. There's iron in her, but she's all woman, too."

He walked away from the water, his mind returning to Churupati. Carefully, he assembled what knowledge he possessed, the fragments heard here and there about the renegade. Whatever was done here, and whatever chance of survival they had must be based on that knowledge.

Behind him Jennifer Fair was both angry and confused. She glanced almost resentfully at Junie. What was there about her that was so much? Yet even as she asked herself the question, she knew the answer. The girl had courage, and courage of a rare kind. She had survived a terrible ordeal, and without whining, without even crying. As for herself, Jennifer had to admit, she had been fussing over the inconvenience of living in one of the finest ranch houses in Arizona!

Logan Cates prowled restlessly among the rocks, always careful to avoid exposing himself. Undoubtedly there were little potholes of water out there, and Churupati would find them, and an Indian needed little water. Like a coyote or a chaparral cock, he could go for days on a few swallows.

Yet whatever was to happen could not be long delayed, and for even this delay, Churupati must have a purpose. Logan Cates scowled at the shadows beyond the area of their defense. What was Churupati planning?

EIGHT

Logan Cates came down from the rocks and found a place back from the water's edge where he could roll up in his blankets. The night was cold, the day's heat gone, and a faint breeze stirred from the Gulf, not many miles to the south.

He lay awake, staring up at the stars, trying to find a solution, and then he gave it up and turned on his side and was almost instantly asleep. Yet suddenly he was once more awake, aroused by that sixth sense developed by hunter and hunted. There was movement where there should be none.

Cates held himself very still, straining his ears into the dark. It seemed he had only just fallen asleep, but the stars told him several hours had passed. He waited, sure there had been some slight movement to awaken him, and his eyes searched the rim of the rocks. Suddenly the movement came again, only it was closer.

Near the pool something stirred, and a figure rose slowly and for several seconds remained still. It was a bulky figure, heavier than—it was Big Maria!

There was no reason for her not to be there, no reason why she should not be moving around, but there was something so surreptitious about her actions that he watched closely. She held her saddlebags in her hands, and she moved by him

58

in moccasins that made no sound. Like an Indian she slipped by him into lava rocks south of the pool, and as she disappeared he heard a faint clink of metal on metal.

He started to rise and follow, then hesitated. Whatever she was doing she did not wish to be seen, and whatever it was could not be important to him . . . or could it?

He was still worrying about that when she returned, and now the saddlebags were gone!

Those saddlebags had been heavy for her and she was a very strong woman. She had been quick to take them from her horse so they would not be handled by anyone but herself. And now she had taken those saddlebags and concealed them. It all began to weave a curious and interesting pattern . . . who was Big Maria? Where had she come from, if not Tucson? Where could she have come from that would allow her horse to arrive comparatively fresh? Where could she have been that would still allow her time to have been in Tucson when Jim Fair arrived searching for Jennifer?

He told himself that it was no business of his, but then he began to remember that sack . . . what could be so heavy but gold? And what but gold could she be hiding out in the rocks? Had anybody seen her but him?

For several minutes he lay awake, then dozed off, and when next his eyes opened there was a faint gray in the sky, and he came to his feet at once and crossed to the lower pool, where he bathed his face and hands then dried himself with his neckerchief. He combed his hair with his fingers and put on the black hat.

Beaupre crossed to him. "All quiet." He struck a match to his cigarette and glanced at Cates out of the corners of his eyes. "How far is it to the Gulf? I mean, could a man make it, d' you s'pose?"

"Maybe three days from here, maybe a bit more. If a man made it he would need a good horse, lots of water, and a very special kind of luck. There's no water south of here, and no people except Seri Indians."

"Might be a way out," Beaupre suggested.

"Not a chance!" Logan Cates found himself wondering who had suggested the route to Beaupre. "Whatever water you had, you'd have to carry along. There isn't enough in any canteen to get a man through, and when he got there what would he do?"

"Catch himself a boat."

"Just like that? Few boats come up that far, and fewer still come close to the east shore. No, Jim, you'll have to think of something else."

Beaupre was obviously unconvinced, and Cates watched him as he walked away. A man would be a fool to attempt such a ride. The country was bleak desert, sand dunes and broken lava, without water, without any settlements, not even a ruined ranch. There was no more desolate land under the sun than that around Pinacate. But somebody had given Jim Beaupre the idea.

To attempt to find another way out than that to Yuma was a waste of time. The desert to the south was a death trap that offered nothing, and their only hope was to make a stand here, and while making the stand attempt to locate the Indian camp. Once located they could make a counterattack and might deal them such a blow as to render them harmless for the future. In the meanwhile they were secure, or reasonably so.

Yet their greatest enemy was not the Apaches, but the trouble that lay among themselves and the strain of waiting for an attack that seemed never to come.

Logan Cates climbed among the rocks. It was very still, and upon the wide face of the desert nothing moved. Even now, surrounded by Indians, in danger of attack at any moment, able to trust no rock or bush, Logan Cates loved the desert morning. The stillness, the distance, the far blue serrated ridges, the lonely peaks, and over all the vast and empty sky.

Nothing moved out there, not even a lizard. Yet the very silence was a menace, the stillness a warning. If they had been east of Tucson, or even closer to the town, there might be a chance of help; here there was none. Whatever future they had they must provide for themselves. And then he remembered the mysterious movements of Big Maria.

A stir of movement caught his eye and he eased his Winchester higher, alert and ready.

Nothing happened.

Yet behind that brush there had been something, something alive.

Where could she have hidden the gold, if gold it was? She had been gone only a few minutes, and could not have gone far, nor would she wish to chance being captured by Indians or being missed. Yet in this broken country of lava rock there were a million places. Everywhere there were cracks, hollows, tumbled broken rock. He had heard no sound, and if she had covered it, that meant there would have been a rattle of stones that he could have heard at the distance she could have gone. It must, then, be lowered into a crack or tucked into a hollow.

Smoke began to rise from the stirred-up fire, and glancing down he was surprised to see it was not Junie Hatchett, but Jennifer.

Zimmerman was walking toward the fire, his rifle in the hollow of his arm, and Big Maria was brushing her hair into place with her hands. Logan Cates considered her for a moment. She was a dangerous woman, big, strong as a man and hard as nails.

His eyes scanned the terrain out before them. There was good shelter there. It was a place where they might get close enough for a rush, and he had just seen movement there. On a sudden hunch he turned quickly, and catching Lonnie Foreman's eye, held up four fingers.

Lonnie hesitated, then realizing what Cates wanted, he grabbed Zimmerman, Kimbrough, Conley and Styles. The four moved swiftly up to the rocks and Logan Cates scattered them into position facing the danger area. They settled down, guns ready.

Beaupre, aroused from partial sleep by the movement, picked up his rifle and joined them. Hidden behind rocks and in brush, they waited. Minutes ticked by, and nothing happened; the morning was still cool and pleasant, the desert was innocent of movement. Nothing stirred out there, not even a dust-devil. And there was no sound.

Ten minutes, twenty minutes passed. A fly buzzed near and lit on a rock just ahead of Cates. He was getting stiff from holding his position.

Half an hour went by and the waiting men were growing restless. A bird lit in the brush some fifty feet away and began preening his feathers. Down at the fire the breaking of branches for fuel made loud sounds in the still morning. Big Maria and Jennifer were talking, their voices carrying clearly to the watching men.

Cates cleared his throat soundlessly and drew a deep breath. Zimmerman was getting out his tobacco and the tops of the western peaks were growing yellow and pink from the rising sun. Lonnie yawned and shifted his position a little. The bird suddenly took off, flying straight up and then away, and the Apaches came with a rush.

They started out of the sand and brush where nothing had seemed to be, and they were not thirty yards from the line of defense in the lava rocks. They had been expecting one guard, at most two, and they ran head on into a withering blast of fire. Logan Cates fired at Churupati, whom he saw plainly, and the bullet missed, knocking down an Indian behind him. And then the Apaches were in the rocks and it was hand to hand and every man for himself.

An Apache came over the rocks almost as Cates's first shot sounded. He grabbed at Cates's rifle barrel and Cates kicked him in the groin, then swung the rifle barrel sidewise and caught the Indian across the skull. He fired instantly at another, saw him stagger, and then suddenly they were gone and there was nothing in sight but a couple of trails of blood on the sand where Indians had been shot down and dragged away.

They were gone . . . even the one he had slugged with the rifle barrel. Somehow he had rolled over and lost himself in the rocks. There was nothing to indicate there had been an attack but the trails of bloody sand, the acrid smell of gunsmoke in the clear morning air, and Styles.

Styles was down, an arrow in his chest. Lonnie was sitting sidewise, his back to a boulder, bandaging a burned wrist.

"How many'd we get?" Conley wondered.

"Two, three," Cates replied. "Maybe three or four wounded."

"How'd you guess they were comin'?" Foreman asked.

"Hunch . . . saw a bush move, figured maybe this was the place and time."

"And what now?" Kimbrough asked, watching Zimmerman lift the wounded Styles to carry him to the fire.

"We wait, and watch the horses. They'll try for them again now."

Beaupre had gone back to his bedroll. The desert was still. Jennifer climbed the rocks with a cup of coffee and a piece of beef. Squatting on his heels, Cates ate hungrily.

Conley and Kimbrough had waited. Lonnie finished bandaging his wrist and took the coffee Jennifer offered him.

"What chances have we?" Jennifer asked.

"Better than even, I'd say, if we sit tight."

"Can they get at us?"

"If we let down for a minute, they'll be in here."

Conley got up. "I'll go down with the horses." He ducked from rock to rock, drew one bullet, seemingly from out of nowhere, but grinned over his shoulder at them as he dropped from sight, heading for the arroyo.

Zimmerman climbed back up to the rocks. He moved with ease despite his size, handling himself without effort. Squatting down, he stuffed his pipe. His jowls were black with beard. "Styles's losin' blood," he said. "I think he's had it."

"Big Maria's working on him," Lonnie said.

"Yeah." Zimmerman struck a light and drew deep on the pipe. "Notice them saddlebags of hers? Mighty heavy, I'd say."

Kimbrough glanced at him "None of our business," he said.

"Maybe. And maybe I'm curious. Bags that heavy—I'd say they'd have gold in 'em. Maybe they would."

63

Nobody said anything, and Logan Cates kept his eyes busy searching the desert. He might have guessed Zimmerman would have noticed. There would be trouble now. To a man obviously out of tune with the Army, as Zimmerman was, the gold would offer an escape route.

There was a burst of firing from the direction of the horses, then silence. Later, there was a single shot from where Lugo lay among the rocks.

The sun was up. It was going to be a hot day. Taylor crawled up beside them. "Water's dropped," he said. "Two inches, anyway. Anybody think about that? There's a lot of us here, there's the horses. We use a lot. It won't last forever."

Logan Cates had been thinking about that water. All three tanks were wider at top than at bottom. The lower tank where the horses were watered was very shallow, and although there was water in the other tanks, they had a large party, considering the source of supply, and the water would not last forever.

Could they outlast the Apaches? Knowing them, Cates had no desire to try, and yet there might be no alternative. Zimmerman was hatching some idea in that heavy brain of his, Taylor was surly, and Beaupre was watching Taylor like the tough old wolf he was. Trouble could break loose at any moment. As for Big Maria, she made Cates uneasy, and he could not tell exactly why.

The sun was higher now, and it was hot. He mopped sweat from his brow and cursed the heat, the dust, and the situation, cursed under his breath, for whatever happened he must not let them see anything but a good face and a confident one.

"I wish they'd attack," Kimbrough said.

Cates glanced at him. A little of the polish was gone. Without a shave he looked irritable and somehow weaker than he had. The clothes that had been so dressy now looked worse than his own, and somehow it made the whole man seem shabby, down-at-heel.

The heat waves shimmered in the distance and overhead a lone buzzard wheeled, waiting.

NINE

Styles was dying, and he was delirious. They all knew he was dying, and by now the Apaches knew it also. Sometimes he cried out, his voice rising in a thin, wavering wail in the still, hot air of the desert. Junie sat beside him, putting damp cloths on his brow and sponging his face at intervals.

Grant Kimbrough paced restlessly. His coat was thrown aside and his shirt sleeves rolled up. The gun he wore was visible now and Logan Cates noticed it thoughtfully. It was a gun that had seen much use. Kimbrough's face was haggard and he was unshaven. There was an impatience in him that had not been obvious before.

The heat, the waiting, the expectation of attack and the cries of the dying man were affecting them all. Overhead the buzzard had been joined by another . . . they swept in wide, loose circles against the heat-glazed sky. Nothing happened.

Kimbrough turned suddenly on Cates. "We've got to get out of here!" He was almost shouting. "We can't stay any longer!"

"Sorry."

Kimbrough glared at him, then strode away, his back stiff with fury.

Jennifer came to him from near the fire. "Logan," her

use of his first name startled him, "there's not much food left."

"How much?"

"Enough for today, and a little for tomorrow."

He should have been thinking of that. Nobody had carried much food and they had been stretching it out as far as possible. That it had lasted this long was surprising, and at least partially due to the fact that there was too much else to worry about and so nobody had eaten more than a few bites. It was necessary to maintain a constant watch. Their position was secure only so long as they were vigilant, for they were in the arroyo and once an Apache was able to reach the edge of it all their positions became untenable.

So then . . . they might have to make a run for it after all.

How slim their chances would be once they left this trough in the rocks he well knew. Beaupre and Lugo knew also, and Sheehan. How much the others knew he could only guess, but Kimbrough, Taylor and Zimmerman all wanted to be moving. Yet once in the open, tied down by the few horses they had, they would be sitting ducks for the Apaches. All the Indians needed to do was hang off on their flanks and pick them off as opportunity offered.

No . . . they must stay here.

Even as he made the decision, he kept his mind open, hoping for a chance, for some other way out.

South, as had been suggested? But what then? There was no place to go for many, many miles. Only an empty, deserted shore, sandy and miserable with intense heat, doubtful water supplies and only the faint hope of sighting a fishing boat from the south or a steamer headed for the mouth of the Colorado.

"Well," Zimmerman asked, "what do we do? Stay here and starve, or make a run for it?"

Grant Kimbrough glanced up at him from his seat by the fire, his face expressionless. "Yes, leader," there was a tinge of sarcasm in his voice, "we'd like to know. What do we do now?"

"We sit tight."

"Damn it, man!" Taylor sprang to his feet. "Are you crazy? We'll all starve to death or be picked off one at a time, like that poor soldier! I move we hit the desert and hit running!"

"What about the women?" Cates asked mildly.

Taylor's eyes shifted, and he looked angry, but he was a stubborn man. "I move we run for it," he said.

"How much chance would we have in the open?" Cates asked. "Not much, I'd say. And how much water could we carry?"

"I'm ready to go any time," Webb said. "I don't believe there's more than half a dozen 'Paches out there."

"We stay," Cates said. "We sit tight."

"You stay!" Zimmerman was ugly. "I'm goin' and I'm goin' now!"

"And I'll go with him!" Webb declared.

"If you go," Cates said, "you'll have to walk. No horses are leaving here."

Zimmerman turned slowly. He looked at Cates with a slow, measuring glance. "I say I'll ride out of here," he said softly, "and I think I'll ride that zebra dun."

Grant Kimbrough leaned back on his elbow, a faintly amused expression on his face.

Sheehan, Beaupre and Lugo were away on watch or sleeping. Lonnie Foreman was up in the rocks. Those who remained were against him, except perhaps the women. Logan Cates stood flatfooted, his feet a little apart. He was going to have to kill Zimmerman . . . he could see it coming and he did not want to do it. The big soldier started forward and Webb moved a little to the left and Logan Cates stepped back a little, his hand poised over his six-shooter. "I'd get back if I were you," he said coolly. "I don't want to kill either of you. We need you."

"We don't need you!" Zimmerman said, grinning. "And you won't draw."

"That's right," Kimbrough said quietly, "he won't."

It was unexpected . . . Kimbrough's pistol covered Cates. "Grant!" Jennifer cried out. "No!"

67

"They're right, Jennifer," Kimbrough said, "we've got to ride out of here. It's our only chance. Take his gun, Zimmerman."

"No."

Junie Hatchett had Big Maria's shotgun and she was holding it as if she knew how to use it. The shotgun was aimed at Kimbrough and the range was no more than thirty feet.

"You drop that gun, Mister Kimbrough, and you drop it now. You make yourself a move and I'll cut your head off. The second barrel goes for him." She jerked her head to indicate Zimmerman. "And if you don't think I'll do it, you just hold that pistol until I count two. One, t—"

Kimbrough backed up, his face sullen. "You better not go to sleep, Cates," he said. "If you do, I'll kill you."

"When he's asleep," Junie said, "I'll be awake, mister."

As they moved away, Cates turned to Junie Hatchett. "Thanks," he said simply.

She glanced at him. "If anybody can get us out of here," she said, "it'll be you."

Jennifer looked after her as the girl returned to the fire. "I see what you meant," Jennifer said. "There *is* iron in her." She hesitated. "Do you think she would have shot Grant?"

Cates nodded grimly. "She'd have shot him. She would have done just what she said she would, and what's more, they both knew it. Her finger was taking up slack when he dropped that pistol."

"I can't understand it," Jennifer said, frowning. "What could have come over Grant?"

Logan Cates let his eyes wander along the edges of the arroyo. "Maybe he got carried away," Cates suggested dryly. "It's times like this that bring a man face to face with himself."

The sun flared like a burnished sword and the sky was like a white-hot sheet of steel. Around them the lava grew too hot to touch and they led the horses to water, and returned them again to the thin shade in the lower arroyo. During all this time the desert stirred with no sound, the Apaches gave no indication of their presence and no quail called nor did the wind

68

blow, nor did any stone rattle in the parched silence. The thirsty sky drank of the pools, and the people at the water holes drank, and the water seemed to fall away beneath them.

In the late afternoon a restless Conley, tired of sitting and watching where nothing was, lifted his head a little to peer at a cluster of rocks and brush. The report of the rifle was thin in the great silence and distance, a little, lost sound in the emptiness. The young soldier fell, tumbling down among the rocks, and there lay still.

Jennifer was first to reach him, then Big Maria and Cates. Maria looked up. "Just burned him," she said. "He'll be all right."

Cates descended into the lower arroyo. Beaupre was resting in the shade. Lugo was crouched immovable against a rock face. Cates squatted beside him. "What d' you think? How many are out there?"

Tony Lugo shrugged. "I think twenty . . . more, maybe. I think Churupati won't attack with less."

"We need food," Cates said. "I'll try it tonight."

"You get kill."

"No." Cates indicated a thin spot in the brush near the base of a smoke tree. "I go down the arroyo, tell nobody but you. I can go like an Indian. With the glasses I have seen some mountain sheep south of here. They want to come for water and they wait to see if we will go away. I think I can find them."

"They'll hear the gun."

"No. I'm going to use a bow and arrow. I have used them many times when I lived among the Cheyenne."

"I make. You let me go."

"No, I'll go. But you can make it. If I started, they would be wondering why. I don't want anyone to know where I am, you understand?"

The need for food was serious. A few days might make all the difference, and Logan Cates knew that by now there was doubt in Yuma. The sheriff's posse had not returned, and already there would be talk of sending out another group to find the first . . . or their bodies.

The disappearance of the soldiers at the same time would immediately alert the people at Yuma to the probability of an Indian attack. All travel from the east would have ceased also, and these indications would be sufficient to allow them to understand what had happened. There were not enough men at the Fort to send out an expedition, but combined with what civilians could be sent out there would be a good-sized party.

There was every chance for survival if they could wait the Indians out. Up to now the fight was all on the side of the defending party. Styles was dying—he had even ceased to cry out now—but otherwise they were still a formidable fighting force if he could keep them together, and their position was excellent. Despite the falling of the water, there was enough for several days even if the terrible heat continued. It was far over a hundred degrees, but with food they could make it.

The mountain sheep, a type of bighorn slightly different from those far to the north, were excellent eating, and it was likely they had never been hunted. He had noticed them on the ridges looking toward the wells several times, and they might still be there.

If he could get a sheep there was a good chance they could last out the week. By that time there might be a relief expedition sent out. It was true that such a force would be likely to go along the route to the north, but when they reached Bates Well and found it dry, then there would be time to start putting two and two together. In Yuma they knew of Papago Wells, and they would come south and find them. Everything depended on keeping the party intact.

He dared not let Zimmerman realize he was absent or the big soldier would be stirring up trouble. Sheehan would try to keep him in line, but tough as the sergeant was, he would be no match for the younger tougher Zimmerman.

It was well after dark when Logan Cates made his move. Kimbrough was on watch in the rocks, and Lonnie was asleep.

Zimmerman had turned in also, lying near Big Maria, yet far enough off so she would not be suspicious. The other men were scattered on watch or sleeping, and Cates had told no one but Lugo what he intended to do.

He left his pistol, and took only the bow, half a dozen arrows and his Bowie knife.

Lying flat, he eased his way under the lowest limbs of the smoke tree and into the rocks. When there he lay still for several minutes, listening. Then with infinite care he snaked down into the rocks and out on the edge of the sand. Again he paused to listen. When half an hour had passed he was no more than fifty yards from the barricade, and he had seen no one. Then, just as he was about to move, there was a subdued rustle of movement.

Not ten feet from him a dark form moved from the shadow of some brush and started up the wash toward the barricade. Waiting until the Indian had gone on, Cates rose soundlessly from the ground and moved out.

Another hour passed, and then he saw the first of the bighorns. He heard it before he saw it, heard it cropping grass upwind of him but against the side of a bluff and invisible. Notching an arrow, he settled back to wait. He was close. The slightest sound might startle the bighorn into a run, and it might be impossible to get so close to another, so he would not move. He would not move at all.

The minutes ticked slowly by, and several times he heard the movement of the bighorn's feet on rock. Yet he could see nothing. Yet, on his left there was a place where the bluff fell away and when the sheep got that far he would be skylined.

He waited. Over the bluff in the distance there was a lone star hanging in the dark sky. He heard the bighorn step lightly, and then other sound—it was another sheep, further back. Or was it?

He held very still, listening. Somewhere, not a dozen feet away, he could hear the faint breathing of another man! He hesitated, and suddenly the sheep moved and Cates heard the sharp *twang* of a bowstring, heard the thud of the arrow

71

striking home and the startled grunt of the bighorn! The sheep lunged, then fell to its knees and rolled over, the horns striking on the rock with a metallic sound. Instantly, an Indian arose from the rocks and started forward.

For a breathtaking instant the Indian was himself outlined, and Logan Cates turned his bow, loosed his arrow and missed! In the instant of turning some sound had warned the Apache for he turned swiftly and instantly sprang at Cates. Knocked over backwards by the hurtling body, Cates could only throw up his knees to protect his stomach. The Indian struck them with his body and Cates threw him off with a convulsive jerk, then rolled over, drawing his knife as he rolled.

The Apache struck at him, and Cates felt the whisper of the razor-sharp blade as it missed his ear and cut sharply into his shirt. At the same time, Cates struck a wicked left-handed blow into the Indian's belly. The Apache was knocked back by the blow, almost winded, and they both came to their feet together.

Cates cut wickedly with the knife, felt it strike and glance off, and then they were tied in a clinch and something warm, wet and slippery was making his hands fight for their grip. The Indian broke free and backed off a step, and Cates followed, crouching, holding his knife low with the cutting edge up, ready to strike for the soft lower part of the Indian's body.

They circled warily, and then the Indian attacked. He came in low, the knife gleaming bright in the starlight, and Cates caught the blow with his own heavier blade, the two clashing as they came together. Then, even as the blades clashed, Cates stepped in and jerked the knife up with all his strength. It slid off the Indian's blade and plunged into his body.

The Apache gave a hard gasp, and said something, too low for Cates to distinguish, then slid to the sand. From the choking, gurgling sound Cates knew the man was dying. He backed away from him, then looked around to orient himself. He must find the bighorn, cut it up and get back as swiftly as possible.

It was a blaze of white on the animal's belly that guided him to it. Swiftly, he skinned the sheep, working fast in the darkness, and working by touch. Gathering the two hind-quarters, the saddle and every available bit of meat he could get in the few minutes he had to work, Cates bundled it all into the hide and straightening up, bow and arrows in hand, he started back.

For several minutes he hurried, trying not to stumble, fighting for breath, and then he found the arroyo. There he paused for several minutes, listening. He remembered the Indian who had gone up the arroyo as he came down it—that Indian would probably still be there. Shifting the burden to his left hand, which also gripped the bow and arrows, Cates drew his knife again and started up the wash, expecting at every step to be attacked.

It was very still as he worked his way through the jungle of growth in the bottom of the wash. From time to time he paused to listen, then moved forward again. Once a branch caught in the hide of the sheep and *twanged* sharply as it pulled free.

Hastily, he took three quick steps and crouched low, waiting and listening. Off to his left he heard a faint whisper of sound as of buckskin rubbing together or a moccasin in the sand. He moved again, quickly, then paused to listen.

He was sure he was almost at the place where he had left the oasis and he eased his burden of meat to the ground. For a long time he held his breath, listening. Despite the coolness of the night, he was sweating. He shifted the knife to his left hand and rubbed the right palm on his shirt. On one knee, he rested.

An hour earlier, Grant Kimbrough had come down from the rocks and walked to the fire. Beaupre had relieved him and nobody else was moving around. He glanced at the bundled figures on the ground and tasted the scalding coffee. If any of them got out of this alive, they would be lucky.

How had he ever gotten himself into such a predicament? They should never have stopped, but kept running. Long ago they would have been in Yuma, and from there a man could buy passage to San Francisco, or go by stage over the Butterfield route.

San Francisco! The lights of the city seemed something that had never been, something beyond belief now. That was the life, not this. And old Jim Fair would come to terms. He had nobody but Jennifer and he would want her to have the best. The thing to do was to get out now, to awaken Jennifer, saddle their horses and make a run for it.

The thought came to him suddenly, and he tried to dismiss it, but it returned to his mind. Well, why not? It was doubtful that more than two or three Apaches would be on watch. They would be sure by now that none of the party would make a break.

But how to get the horses out? He considered that, dismissing as impossible all ways but one. A man would have to go down the draw, make an opening in that wall of brush and get out that way. It could be done. From Yuma they could send help, and in the meantime they would be on their way to San Francisco.

Kimbrough looked at the dark brown coffee, swirling it in his cup. He had only seventy dollars in his pocket, and it was not enough. Of course, if he could get in a game in Yuma—and they could sell their horses.

He glanced at the place where Jennifer slept. Would she go? She'd be a fool not to, and the chance they took would be slight. Still, if there was one more man . . . he thought of Zimmerman, then dismissed it. He did not like the big, overbearing soldier; he was a dangerous man.

Webb was another story . . . or Conley. But Conley leaned toward Cates and might not go.

Cates . . . where was Logan Cates?

Kimbrough came suddenly to his feet. Cates was gone. He had not seen the man for hours. Hastily, Kimbrough went from bundle to bundle, checking. All there but those on guard, and Cates.

He had given them the slip—he was gone. Instantly, Kimbrough felt a sharp anger. Cates had gone and left them behind! What kind of a man was that? Hearing a crunch of a boot on the sand, Kimbrough turned sharply. It was Sergeant Sheehan.

"Cates is gone, Sergeant," Kimbrough said; "he pulled out and left us."

Sheehan's head came up sharply. "I don't believe it!"

"Nevertheless, he's gone. Look and see for yourself."

"Nonsense, man! He wouldn't—"

Kimbrough laughed without humor. "Nonetheless, he's gone. And if we're smart, we'll all go. We can make it. I think we could make Yuma, all right, and I don't believe there are so many Indians out there. If we put a bold face on it, run for it—"

Sergeant Sheehan measured Kimbrough coolly. "Mister, you're forgetting something. We have fourteen people here, and just eight horses."

Grant Kimbrough started to speak, then stopped. Slowly, the excitement went out of him. Fourteen people and eight horses. "But one of those horses is mine," he said.

Sheehan nodded shortly. "That it is," he said, and turning abruptly, he walked away.

TEN

Webb was standing close behind him when Kimbrough turned around. Webb was a man of thirty, burned red by the sun. "We're fools," Webb was saying, "pure damn fools! I say we ought to take the horses and run for it. If the others want to stay, let 'em. They can have it."

"We couldn't do that," Kimbrough said, but his words carried no conviction, no force. He had been thinking of doing just what Webb suggested, for he did not want to die, nor did he want to remain here in the heat with no bath, no chance to shave, no change of clothing. It was no way for a gentleman to live. He wanted to take Jennifer and get out—fast.

Webb would be the man to help. He was not dangerous as Zimmerman was, but a follower, a man who would never act by himself. "No," Kimbrough repeated, "it wouldn't be right."

"I'd rather be a live coward," Webb replied shortly.

Coward. The word stiffened Kimbrough, shocked him. Immediately he began to reason. It would not be cowardice for he had never wanted to stay, but to ride on, and to ride on might be more dangerous than staying. And he had nothing in common with these people, nor did he wish to have. He had allowed himself to be persuaded and now he would merely resume his original course. It was simple as that.

76

"What about it?" Webb persisted. He stepped closer to Kimbrough, and the gambler started to draw back in distaste, then held himself. "Why shouldn't we go?" Webb insisted. "There'd be more food and water for the others."

Kimbrough turned away. "Later," he said. "We'll see."

He walked swiftly away to the fire, which was the focal point of all their living these days. Men came and went from the fire for it was the center of their lives, of their being. They drank coffee, even if it was now more than half mesquite bean coffee, they drank coffee and sat, for there was nothing else to do.

The sky was growing pale now, pale lemon and gray, and the rocks were black, the red rock of the lava and the black rock of other flows. Soon the sun would rise and it would be hot, it would be open and clear and everyone would be visible, and there would be no chance for escape.

Still no sign of Cates.

Jennifer stirred under her blanket, then sat up, brushing her hair back. Even now, after these brutal days in the desert, she still looked lovely, still seemed fresh. A bit drawn, but still beautiful.

"He's gone," Kimbrough said, "Cates is gone."

"Gone?" She looked at him, trying to realize what the word meant. "Cates? No."

"He's gone, I tell you. You'll see." Suddenly he was speaking with almost savage triumph. "He talked so much about staying, about sitting tight. Then he took off himself, without so much as a word."

"I don't believe it!" Jennifer was suddenly on her feet. "He wouldn't do a thing like that. He's no coward."

Coward. That word again. Grant Kimbrough stared at her, almost with animosity. "Maybe he's just smart. That's what we all should have done."

"He hasn't gone," Jennifer was suddenly sure. "Logan Cates would not leave us, I know he would not. He isn't that kind of man."

Big Maria was sitting up. She stared around her, then

hunched herself to her feet. She was very heavy and she had made no effort to comb her hair or straighten her clothing. Her eyes seemed to have grown harder, and they looked from Jennifer to Kimbrough and then up at the rocks.

They were all coming around now. Junie was brushing her hair back into place, trying with ineffectual hands to brush her dress into some semblance of shape.

"Cates is gone," Kimbrough said again.

Junie looked her contempt and walked away from the group.

Jim Beaupre picked up the battered coffee pot. "He was gone, all right, but now he's back."

They all looked at him, and Beaupre took his time. "He's back with enough sheep to keep us all eating a couple of days . . . if we go easy."

"I don't believe it," Kimbrough said. "He's gone and that's what we all should do—leave."

There was a stir on the edge of the group. They parted to see him standing there, with the blood of the Indian he had killed staining his shoulder and shirt and a thin red scratch along his cheek from the knife blade. He did not know it was there, had not felt it when it happened to him.

He dropped the skin packed with chunks of meat and said, "I'm not gone and nobody's going. The one chance we've got is to stay right here."

"Maybe," Kimbrough's anger suddenly flared; "maybe I'll go whether you like it or not."

Cates merely looked at him. "All right," he said, "go ahead. Go any time you like, but you'll have to walk."

Kimbrough had started to turn away, then wheeled back. "Walk?" He took an angry step toward Cates. "I'll be damned if I'll— Why should I walk? I'll ride the horse I came with."

"You'd deserve him," Cates replied coolly. "That horse won't make it to Yuma . . . but he'll make it part way, so you're not taking him. He's community property now."

Grant Kimbrough stood very still, his hands at his sides. There was one thing Cates did not know: that he, Kimbrough, was a fast man with a gun, probably one of the very fastest. Kimbrough was thinking of that now. He knew he could kill Cates and knew this was as good a time as any.

"You'd try to take my horse from me?" he asked.

"All the horses here, mine included," Cates replied, "now belong to the group until we get out of here. The strong must walk, the weak will ride, and at least one horse must be kept for carrying water alone. No man or woman has a right to a horse of his or her own now."

"We didn't agree to that," Taylor objected.

"I'm sorry," Cates replied, "but it's necessary." He gestured toward the meat, changing the subject. "We'd best cook that. It won't keep in this heat."

Abruptly he walked away. His weariness hit him suddenly and when he found a shady spot he sat down heavily. With an effort he managed to get his boots off, and, lying down, was asleep at once.

"Takes a lot on himself, doesn't he?" Webb muttered.

Grant Kimbrough did not reply, but he was filled with impotent anger. Their only hope lay in flight, and if he had not crossed the desert to the west he was sure that a man on a good horse could make Yuma in no time. Without the drag of those who must walk, and those other women, they could make it through on fast horses.

Getting out of the cul-de-sac that was their defensive position was the big thing. Once away they could run for it, and Webb was ready to go. So he would plan it that way, prepare Jennifer to be ready for the break, and when opportunity came they would ride out. If Cates objected, Kimbrough would kill him. He had, he realized, been giving the contingency a lot of thought these past two days.

The first thing was to talk to Jennifer. She would, he was sure, be only too anxious to go.

Logan Cates awakened with a start. He was bathed in perspiration and for a moment he did not know where he was. A blanket had been stretched from the rock to the ground

79

forming a crude shelter that allowed shade and some air circulation. He sat up, and listened . . . there was a crackle from the fire, a distant murmur of voices, the sound of someone stirring about close by.

He checked his pistols. These actions, the moment of listening to judge what was happening around him, the checking of the guns, all were second nature to him now. When he slid out from behind the blanket curtain he resumed the boots that he had immediately put on again after returning from his midnight foray.

Jennifer was at the fire. "You slept a long time," she said. "It's noon."

"Anything happen?"

"Styles is dead."

"He's better off, but it's a hard thing to die here."

"Why did you go out last night? You might have been killed."

"We needed meat."

"What happened out there?"

"Met an Apache whose luck had run out."

Big Maria had moved herself closer to the rocks, near the place where Cates had seen her disappear that night. She kept a gun close to her at all times, and before Cates had finished his coffee he could see by her actions that she was suspicious and ready for trouble.

He must talk to Lonnie Foreman. The boy was solid, he had nerve, and he was a stayer. He could count on Foreman, probably Sheehan. Who else? Junie Hatchett, with perhaps Beaupre and Lugo. Conley was another question but he seemed to be a solid citizen. As to Jennifer. . .

Lugo was at the fire, gnawing on a mutton bone. He glanced up at Cates and his eyes went to the bloody shirt. It was like the Pima that he made no comment, asked no questions. The bloody shirt spoke for itself, and the Indian is not one to talk of the obvious or of needless things. Lugo knew there had been a fight out there in the dark, the fact that

Logan Cates had returned and that the blood was not his own was sufficient evidence as to the outcome.

"Who's with the horses?" Cates asked.

"Kimbrough," Lugo said. "He watch horses."

Logan Cates considered that but saw nothing in it that was dangerous. It was true that Kimbrough had always held a position in the rocks or in the brush along the edge of the arroyo, but there were no assigned positions, and a man could choose his own.

"Is he alone?"

"A soldier is with him."

Lonnie Foreman was hunched in the shade talking to Junie. He was stripped to the waist and Junie was mending a rent in his shirt. Beaupre and Zimmerman were digging a grave for Styles in the lower arroyo not far from where the horses were. Webb paced restlessly; Kimbrough was busy with his own thoughts. Logan Cates picked up his Winchester, checked the load and then climbed up in the rocks, noting the water level as he went by. Although the water had fallen considerably since their arrival, there was still enough . . . if they did not stay too long.

Conley was on watch in the rocks. "Nothin'," he said, "just nothin' at all. I never seen so much of nothin'."

Heat waves shimmered and the buzzards, high against the brassy sky, described long, loose circles. Nothing else moved. Cates sat down on a rock and mopped the sweat from his face. His clothing smelled of stale sweat and dust and his eyes were tired of the endless glare of sun on sand and rock. He laid the Winchester across his knees and swore softly.

"My sentiments," Conley said. "I can't figure why I ever come to this country. My folks had them a good farm back in Kentucky. Right nice place . . . used to be parties or dances every Saturday night, and folks come from miles around. Now here I am stuck in a rocky desert with every chance I'll lose my hair. Why does a body come to this country?"

Cates took out the makings and began to build a cigarette.

81

Sweat got in his eyes and they smarted. "You got me, soldier, but you stay a while and it grows on you."

"Not on me. If I get out of this fix I'm takin' off. I'm goin' to those gold fields and find myself a job. I know a fellow in Grass Valley . . . Ever hear a nicer name? Grass Valley. Makes a man think of cool, green meadows an' streams. Maybe it ain't like that, but I'd sure like to give it a try."

Logan Cates lifted the cigarette to touch the edge of the paper to his tongue when he saw the movement. He dropped the cigarette and swung the Winchester. All he saw was a flickering movement and Conley's body jerked sharply. He turned half around as if to speak to Cates, then fell, tumbling over and over among the rocks as Cates's own shot followed the sound of the shot that killed Conley.

Cates fired and saw his bullet kick sand. He fired again, into the brush, then tried a shot at a shelf of rock hoping for a ricochet into the concealed position from which the Indian had fired.

On the instant, all were alert. Beaupre had run forward, lifting Conley from the rocks as if he were a child. It was no use; the soldier was dead. Two gone. Styles and Conley. How many were to go? Out there again the desert was a silent place, a haunted place.

Zimmerman mopped his face and peered into the brush. When he lifted his hand to brush away the sweat it was trembling.

The death of Conley had shocked them all. It had come so suddenly, and that attractive, pleasant young soldier was smashed suddenly from existence. It was proof enough, if proof was needed, that their every move was watched, that the Apaches had made a tight cordon around them, watching, waiting.

Suddenly the desert had become a place of menace; its very silence was evil, its heat was a threat. The sinking level of the water was obvious to them all, their food was growing less, and the forage for the horses was all but a thing of the past. The horses had eaten the grass down to the roots, sparse as it had been, and they had eaten the leaves and the mesquite beans.

The faces of the men were taut, sullen, and frightened, as they waited in place, staring at the blinding glare of the sun-blasted sand and waiting for a target that never appeared.

Even Sergeant Sheehan was feeling the pressure. He looked drawn and old now, and his square shoulders sagged a little. "They'll get us all, Cates," he said. "We're whipped."

ELEVEN

Logan Cates searched the empty desert with his red-rimmed eyes. Nowhere was a sound or a movement. The sun seemed to have spread over the entire sky, and there was no shade. The parched leaves of the mesquite hung lifeless and still, and even the buzzards that hung in the brassy vault above them seemed motionless.

The rocks were blistering to the touch, the jagged lava boulders lay like huge clinkers in the glowing ashes of a burned-down fire. The heat waves drew a veil across the distance. Cates opened his shirt another button and mopped his face with his bandanna. He shifted the rifle in his sweaty hands, and searched the desert for something at which to shoot.

Lonnie Foreman crawled up in the rocks and seating himself, took a healthy pull at his canteen, then passed it to Cates. The water tasted flat and dull, lukewarm from the canteen.

"It's awful down there." Foreman gestured toward the deeper arroyo where the horses were held. "Like an oven."

"They can cover the horses from up higher. Tell 'em to come on up."

Foreman slid off the rocks and when he stood up on the main level he walked slowly away, his boots grating on the rock. He walked past the narrow shelf of shade under which the three women sat. Nobody cared about the fire, nobody wanted coffee. Despite the shortage of food, nobody was even hungry.

Cates watched the men retreat to the higher level. They could watch the horses as well from there, and the defensive position was better. He was afraid of that corral now . . . he could not say why, but it seemed the most vulnerable, and the Apaches would want what horses they could get, either to ride or eat. Pulling the defenders back meant his line of defense was tighter, more compact, better sheltered.

Nothing stirred out there. Now that the men had been pulled back he could hear their conversation. Cates sat quietly among the rocks, ready for anything. Evidently the Apaches had observed the construction of the corral when it was first built, for no attempt had been made to stampede the horses, nor for some time had any effort been made to kill them, so evidently they believed they would have them all before many days had passed.

Nothing moved. From down by the waterhole someone was swearing in a heavy, monotonous voice. A fly buzzed near and lighted on Cates's face. He brushed it with an irritable hand and a bullet spat fragments of granite in his face as the sound went echoing down the hills.

He hunched lower, and, peering between the rocks, tried to find a target. He glanced down to see Zimmerman squatting near Big Maria, whispering. The big woman's face was lowered and Cates could not discern what effect the words were having, if any. They had drawn apart from the others. It was very hot, and very still.

Sheehan found a place in the thin shade and stretched out, trying to rest before the night watch. Kimbrough and Webb sat side by side in the rocks, talking as they kept a lookout.

Logan Cates tried to think of an escape. There had to be a way to get out of here, there was always a way. No matter how he squinted his eyes over the desert and tried to think of some way out, none came to him. By this time, however, the Army knew its patrol was lost or in trouble, and they would know the sheriff's posse was in the same situation. The fact that two well-armed parties had vanished in the same area at the same time was sufficient warning of what must be happening out there. Also, there could have been little or no desert travel in the meantime which would be evidence enough of an Indian outbreak. By this time there would be speculation and un-doubtedly a search party was being organized.

In Tucson, Jim Fair would have given up the search or would by this time have started west, and being the man he was, Cates was quite sure that if Fair realized his daughter had run into trouble, he would be heading west without delay. Nor would they take too long in finding them at Papago Wells. There was, therefore, a double reason for alertness. They must be prepared to warn any search parties of a trap.

Cates began considering a smoke signal . . . yet there was little fuel, and what there was must be conserved until there was absolute necessity.

It was beyond reason that Churupati and his renegades could exist out in those blistering rocks, but they were doing it, and the fact that the slightest incautious movement by the defenders brought a well-aimed shot was evidence enough.

Zimmerman got up suddenly. "To hell with this!" he said suddenly. "I'm gettin' out of here!"

Nobody replied. Lonnie Foreman got up and walked over to the rocks to climb up and relieve Cates. Kimbrough spat into the sand at his feet. His coat had long since been dis-carded and his shirt was torn and dirty. There was a thick stubble of beard on his jaws and his eyes seemed to have thinned and grown mean. They studied Zimmerman now, but he offered no comment.

The big man stood in the center of the open space and glared around him. "I'm ridin' out of here tonight, and any-body who wants to come is welcome!"

Cates reached the ground near him. He turned slowly. "Zimmerman, forget it. We'll all be out of here before long. Just sit tight."

Zimmerman turned sharply around. "When I need advice from you, I'll ask it. I'm ridin' out of here at daylight."

"If you want to leave, just go ahead. But you're not riding."

"No?" Zimmerman measured him with insulting eyes. "You're stoppin' me, I suppose?"

Sheehan was suddenly awake. "Zimmerman!" His voice rang in the space between the walls. "Sit down and shut up!"

Zimmerman did not even turn to glance at Sheehan. He simply ignored the command, his eyes on Cates. "I don't like you, Cates. I never have. All you've done is say 'sit tight.' Well, I'm tired of it, and when I want to ride, I'm ridin', and when I ride, I'm ridin' your horse. What do you think of that?"

Zimmerman took a step nearer. Cates held his ground, his face expressionless. Beaupre was watching him with a kind of fascinated attention, and Grant Kimbrough sat up, curious.

"Sit down, Zimmerman, and forget it. The heat's getting to us all." Logan Cates was cool. "By this time the search parties are preparing. We'll be out of here soon."

"I'll be out when I want to go," Zimmerman said, "but there's something I'm going to do before I leave. I'm going to take that little pistol away from you and—"

Cates struck, and swiftly as he struck, Zimmerman slapped down Cates's left hand with his left, leaving his chin open. Cates's right was a flickering instant behind the left and it struck the bigger man's jaw as the butt of an ax strikes a log. Everybody in the clearing heard the thud of the blow and saw Zimmerman's knees buckle, but the left and right followed so swiftly that Zimmerman hit ground from the force of all blows. He sat stunned and shaken for an instant, while Cates coolly drew back to let him get up. Suddenly, realization seemed to reach Zimmerman and he came off the ground with a lunge and began to close in; his arms were widespread for grasping.

Cates stood very still and let him come and then as Zimmerman lunged, Cates stepped in with a smashing left to the mouth. His lips split, Zimmerman followed through, grabbing at Cates, who turned swiftly inside of the enveloping arms and threw Zimmerman with a rolling hiplock. The big man hit the ground hard. Zimmerman started to rise, and Cates told him, "Don't get up, Zimmerman, or I'll take you apart."

Zimmerman stayed where he was, on his hands and knees, and after a minute Cates walked away to steady himself. He was shaken by the fight. Zimmerman, for all his bulk, knew little of fighting and to have continued would have meant a needless slaughter. Yet he knew with such a man there was never an end. Zimmerman would not forget.

Nobody said anything, and after a while Zimmerman got slowly to his feet and walked to the far end of the arroyo.

"What did you prove?" Taylor asked, looking up at Cates.

Cates ignored the question. "We've got to stay here. It's our only chance. Out in the open, with several of us walking, and women to think of, we wouldn't have a chance. And believe me, that stretch of country from here to Yuma is one of the worst in the world." He turned to Taylor. "You know it is."

"I've been over it before," Taylor declared, "and I can do it again."

"You didn't have women to think of," Cates said, "and you probably had water."

Taylor got up and stalked away to the far side of their area, ignoring the comment. He sat down with Webb and Kimbrough. Big Maria after a moment got up and walked after him. For a moment Logan Cates looked at them, then glanced away.

Lonnie called down from above. "Logan. Somethin' stirrin' up out there!"

He scrambled quickly into the rocks, but the desert showed nothing at all, nothing but the same rocks, the same brush, the same shimmering heat waves, the same—

The arrow came out of the desert from the rocks down near the arroyo, from the rocks out of sight behind the brush that lined it at that place. It came over and it trailed a dark trail of smoke.

"Lugo! Jim! Grab the horses! *Fire!*"

Everyone was on their feet in an instant. The arrow dropped into the brush that formed the corral. There was a brief silence, then a crackle of flame.

Lugo had been quick. He had glimpsed the arrow even as it fell and he made a running dive and scooped sand into the brush and he was lucky. His first scooped double handful lit right on the tiny blaze, and then a second arrow came, and a third. The second was a clean miss, landing in the sand somewhere back of the brush, but the third lit. Beaupre was there now, and Taylor, all desperately throwing sand.

Yet Cates could see from his vantage point that there was no hope. They might extinguish one or a dozen, but the Apaches would keep trying and they would get one arrow where they wanted it. That dry brush would go up like tinder and nothing would be left of the corral.

"Sheehan!" he shouted. "Get the horses up here! Fast!" Sheehan was moving even as Cates yelled and Cates turned swiftly. "Pay no attention to the fire, Lonnie. They may try to attack now!"

Kimbrough had reached the same conclusion and hurriedly got into the rocks to face south toward the lava, his rifle ready. Zimmerman was in the rocks facing north. Suddenly he fired, and then Lonnie fired.

"Missed!" Lonnie said bitterly. "If I could get in just one good shot!"

Cates glanced around at the fire. Another arrow had hit further back, out of reach, and suddenly the wall of brush was swept by roaring, crackling flame. "Back!" he yelled. "Back to the rocks!"

Sheehan, working swiftly with Webb and Jennifer, was already bringing the horses into the rocks, and the others retreated swiftly and fell down in firing positions. The flames roared and the stifling heat beat against their faces, yet they lay still, watching.

The lower tank was lost to them now. With the brush gone the Indians could cover it effectively and there would be no chance to get water from there. And that was the one where the horses had watered. It was low now, little water remained, but enough to have lasted another day, at least. And they must share their water with the horses.

89

Their position was tighter, and it was still strong. It was still a formidable position to attack by any charge, but the net was drawn closer, and there was less room, less water, less food.

For half an hour the brush blazed, then settled down to smoldering, blackened heaps. And overhead the sun blazed from horizon to horizon, and the heat shimmered, and the patient buzzards soared and waited.

Nobody spoke. Their brief efforts in the heat of the sun had left Beaupre and Lugo exhausted. Taylor looked pale, and for once had nothing to say. Each one was impressed with the seriousness of their position, and each realized all the implications.

It was Kimbrough who voiced their feeling. "Now what do we do, Cates? Do we sit tight?"

"We do."

Taylor glared at him; Zimmerman looked his disgust. But it was Beaupre who said, "He's playin' with us, Churupati is; he's playin' with us like a cat plays with a bird. He knows he's got us, he knows we can't get away. He's just havin' himself some fun."

It was hot. There were only thin strips of shade where the rocks cast a slight shadow. The lava caught the blasting heat and reflected it into their faces, for the shade the brush below had offered was gone now. They sat around, stupid with the shock of what had happened, empty of thought.

Without waiting for help, Cates began shifting stones to provide added protection and after a minute or two, Lugo joined him, then Beaupre. Jennifer glanced at Kimbrough but he huddled in deep conference with Webb and Zimmerman and offered no help.

They had water for two, perhaps three days longer; even that meant half rations. Their food was sufficient for three slight meals.

When he climbed back up the rocks, Lonnie glanced at him. "What do we do now?" he asked.

Cates shrugged and tried to huddle into the shade that

was gathering behind a boulder as the sun moved westward. "All we can do is wait. You can bet they aren't having it easy, either." He studied the back of his hand thoughtfully. "I think we might try an attack tonight."

"I want to go."

"Well—maybe." Cates looked up at him. "How are you and Junie making it?"

Lonnie flushed. "She's a mighty nice girl."

"Don't find too many out here."

They sat together, watching the desert. The glare was terrible, although the afternoon was now almost gone, and in the last hours the sun seemed to shine with redoubled intensity. Cates took the glasses and searched the skyline toward Yuma, then that to the east.

Nothing . . . nothing at all.

A bullet clipped rock near his glasses, then another. An arrow, apparently fired at random, came over the rocks and brush and landed near the fire. A third bullet clipped a neat hole in Lonnie Foreman's hatbrim, and another harmless arrow dropped over the rocks.

Cates steadied his rifle and waited. He saw sand slip near the crest of a dune ridge and fired, holding a little low. A hand flew up, seen a moment as it shot high, then slowly lowered. The fingers dug into the sand, clutching a handful, then slowly spreading out as the hand slipped from sight.

"One down," Lonnie said. "That was a good shot."

"It was a lucky shot. I just guessed he might be there."

"Wonder what they're planning out there?"

Cates shrugged. "Who knows? I think Churupati is restless now. He has been expecting us to break and run for it. I think all his planning was for that . . . to get us into the open. We've held them here, they can't have much water, and no Indian wants to leave the rifles and horses they'd get if we ran for it."

Down below in the rocks, Grant Kimbrough got to his feet. "Tonight then?" Webb asked.

"Tonight," Kimbrough replied.

91

TWELVE

Grant Kimbrough had made his decision. The party was doomed, he did not intend to be a part of that doom. For several nights he had been studying a route among the rocks, and he had decided it allowed a safe passage, relatively free of observation, and one over which no sound would be made because of the sand.

Webb could get the horses saddled, and when all was quiet during their watch, they would mount up and slip out. Give them a few miles' start and no Indian pony was going to catch his thoroughbred. They could make it north and then west and they were sure to reach Yuma. On the river as it was, there was no way they could miss, for the Colorado made a moat across the whole west border of Arizona.

Let Logan Cates play his game of sitting tight. He could have it. They would die here, of starvation if not of Indian arrows or bullets. Nobody would come, nobody knew where they were. Zimmerman wanted to come and Zimmerman had some idea of his own . . . all right, let him. Three targets were better than two, and Zimmerman was a big man. In the darkness he was sure to attract most of the gunfire, if there was any, and Kimbrough was sure there would be none.

He walked to where Jennifer was roasting some strips of

mutton. She brushed a wisp of hair back from her face and smiled at him. She had changed in some way he could not define; she seemed more mature, more sure of herself. It was a change that disturbed him, why he could not have said.

"No job for you," he said.

"Somebody has to do it, and Junie does more than her share."

"We'll be out of it soon."

She glanced at him. "I'm glad to hear you say so. I thought you were beginning to think like the others, the ones who believe we'll never get out."

"They may not, but you will."

Her eyes searched his face. "What do you mean by that?"

"That I'm taking care of you, Jen, as I promised I would. I am going to see that you get out of here."

Her eyes softened and she put her hand on his sleeve. "Of course, Grant. I never doubted that you were thinking of me."

"Get some rest," he said; "you'll need it."

He walked away and she saw him go to his horse. He had been rustling extra feed for the thoroughbred these past two days, bringing it to the horse, and picking his hat full of mesquite beans as he lay in the brush.

She made coffee and one by one they came to the fire to eat. Grant was in the best mood she had seen him since their arrival, and she was pleased. Yet when she glanced at Cates she was vaguely uneasy.

Night was drawing near, and the first shadows were creeping out from the rocks, gathering in the hollow spaces, pointing long fingers from the cacti and the ocotillo, but it was a haunted evening. Each in his or her own way was feeling the sudden apprehension, and the Indians who had before seemed closed out now seemed desperately near. The burning of the brush walling the corral had opened a way into their fortress, had deprived them of at least a third of their remaining water, had left them feeling exposed to the dangers of the creeping night.

Nobody talked, and yet nobody slept. All were restless, silent, alert for danger. Fear was a living thing among them.

93

Webb mopped his slack-jawed face with a nervous hand. Taylor's tough assurance was no longer stolid; he moved quickly at the slightest sound, on edge and jittery. Even Jim Beaupre was feeling it. He moved from place to place, studying the desert, eager for a shot at something. Only Tony Lugo seemed the same, and even the Pima was alert. His eyes, which were quiet as a rule, now seemed larger.

They avoided each other's eyes, each haunted by a knowledge they could no longer avoid, that death *was* near, that before another day was gone some of them here might not be alive. The burning of the brush had indicated a change, for it was something the Apaches might have done at any time. If they had not done it until now there had to be a reason.

Grant Kimbrough felt relieved. The very fact that he had made a decision was a relief, and he had no doubt of success. Sure, they were taking a chance, but nothing was going to happen to him, and flight was the only way out now. He would get Jennifer out of this, and they could be married in Yuma.

However, and the thought came to him suddenly, it might not be wise to leave Arizona just yet. If Jim Fair had tried to follow them he might now be dead, killed by the very Indians who lay out there in the rocks. And if that had happened Jennifer might now own all those vast acres and cattle. Yes, it would be wise to marry Jennifer as soon as they reached Yuma.

The plans he had evolved were few and simple. He was soldier enough to know the more complicated the plan the less chance of its working. The horses were close to them; there was a way out into the boulders. Webb, Zimmerman and he would manage to get their horses to that side and under cover of darkness they would ride out and escape. It might be hours before the others realized they were gone. If he considered the fact that they would leave the rocks unguarded it was not for long. In this world one did what was best for one, and what happened to others could not be helped.

Logan Cates, rolling a smoke near the coals of the fire, considered the situation that faced them. Actually, they were better situated for defense now than before, as their lines were tighter. They had almost no food for the horses, and the water was low; there were but eight horses to mount twelve people; and knowing the desert that lay ahead of them, Cates knew that at least one horse must be used to pack water. Otherwise they would never make it at all.

He returned to his thoughts of attacking the Apaches. It had remained in the back of his mind ever since they had been cornered here, but the time must be carefully chosen, and now, he was sure, was the time. At first the Indians would have been too wary, too careful, yet now they would be sure of themselves, they would have settled into a routine, and they would not be expecting the whites to attack.

Too large a party would make too much noise. It might be best if he did it alone, yet such an attack would be less effective. He decided, finally, that it must be three or four men. The selection of Lugo for one of them was immediate. He would be the best of them all on such an attack, and he would refuse to be left behind, anyway. Lonnie would want to go, and the remaining man must be one of the others. He considered Kimbrough, then passed over him. The man had been a horse soldier, no doubt brave enough, but not a man to crawl on his belly in the sand or lie still for what might be hours.

Sheehan must be left behind because if anything happened while they were gone, he was the man to handle it. He wanted no part of Zimmerman or Webb, for he had faith in neither man. It boiled down to Taylor or Beaupre.

When the sun had gone the evening turned the desert into an enchanted place. A soft wind cooled the sands and took away the last of the heat, but it was a wind that just stirred the leaves and was not bold enough to brush branches aside or lift dust. Somewhere far out over the sand a quail called, and the mountains in the west, abandoned by the sun, grew dark with shadow and only the eastern ridges were bright.

Taylor brought fuel to the fire and built it brighter, and Cates strolled to where Lugo sat watching the desert. He squatted on his heels beside the Pima. "Three, four hours from

95

now," he said, "a few of us are going to hit the Apache where it hurts."

"I come," Lugo said. "It is time."

Cates remained, talking quietly with the Pima, telling him what he planned, anxious to get the Indian's reactions. The man was a fighter and he knew the Apache; he would know if the plan was a wise one. But Lugo had no protests, he accepted the suggested route and had only a few comments to make on the probable placing of Apache sentries.

Lonnie was next. The boy was talking to Junie, who was working over the fire, but when she left for a few minutes, Cates explained his purpose. He poked at the fire a bit, then lifted a burning stick to light his cigarette, talking around the cigarette. "You, Lugo and me," he said. "I think one more man."

"You're going to hit their camp?"

"And get a couple of horses, if we can. Maybe four or five."

"That'll be tough."

"Most of all I want to slow them down, make them sick of their job. By now they think we're whipped."

"All right . . . whenever you're ready."

"At eleven, then."

In the last minutes of daylight a sudden smashing volley hit the camp. A bullet knocked the old pot off the fire, another scattered coals. Lonnie hit the ground hard and fired at the brush beyond the margin, and everyone scattered for shelter and firing positions. For a few minutes the fire came thick and fast. One of the horses screamed and reared but miraculously it was only a burn. Beaupre rolled into shelter behind a rock, then scrambled up and raced for a better firing position, and as suddenly the attack was over.

The cooking pot was gone. One of the horses had been creased on the shoulder and Lonnie had had the top of his ear burned, yet they were badly shaken. It seemed unreasonable that the Indians could have been so close and no more serious injuries were sustained.

"Maybe they want us alive," Beaupre said.

Taylor lifted his head slowly and peered at Beaupre. "That's fool talk. Why would they want us alive?"

"We've women here," Beaupre said grimly, "and an Apache can have a sight of fun with a living prisoner."

Taylor's features seemed to alter, his grimness left him, and some of his certainty. He looked from Jim Beaupre to Cates. "They'd never do a thing like that," he said. "Why, that's crazy!"

Yet it was apparent he believed they would. Every person in the southwest had heard stories of what an Apache could do with a living prisoner, and for the first time Taylor seemed to consider that possibility. He lowered his eyes and began trailing sand through his fingers. Nobody else said anything. Junie worked on Lonnie Foreman's ear and Beaupre ran a ramrod through his rifle.

The fire had burned low.

Lugo was rubbing grease in the bullet burn on the horse, and several minutes passed without comment. Kimbrough was thinking of San Francisco . . . once away from here he'd never come back. If Fair was dead, and the ranch was theirs, they'd sell out and go back East. This was no country for a sensible man.

The stars came out, the night wind stilled, somewhere a coyote called. The faint glow from the coals showed on Beaupre's seamed face and glinted from the rifle barrel as he worked. One of the horses stamped and blew. Leaning his head back against a rock, Sergeant Sheehan sang *They're Tenting Tonight On The Old Camp Ground* in a fair Irish tenor. The mournful sound of the song lifted above the little circle among the rocks, and as he sang, Jennifer put sticks on the coals and a little flame began to rise.

The firelight played on their faces and when the song died there was silence.

THIRTEEN

It lacked two hours of midnight and the camp was asleep when Webb finished saddling the horses. He had worked carefully and not a sound had disturbed the sleeping people. Grant Kimbrough was up on the rocks and Zimmerman was somewhere in camp.

Webb had filled Cates's two canteens and a couple of others and they were strapped on one of the horses. He got his own rifle and carried it to Cates's dun horse, which he had selected to ride. The zebra dun had the look of a good horse and it was all he wanted . . . he knew nothing about the dun's nature or that he possessed the disposition of a fiend and the cunning of a Missouri mule.

When he was through he went up into the rocks to Kimbrough. "How's it look?" he whispered.

"Couldn't be better. Not a move down there; still as a grave."

Webb shivered a little, but it might have been the cool air. "Then we're ready, any time," he said.

For a moment longer Kimbrough hesitated. There was in him a queer reluctance to leave his post. He had been a soldier and he knew what it could mean to have a sentry absent from his post; a man who has the lives of others in his trust has no right to sleep, no right to leave that post. Yet this was not the Army, and there had been no trouble at night.

"Where's Zimmerman?"

"Around. He slipped off somewhere."

"All right," Kimbrough had made up his mind. "I'll get Miss Fair."

Webb hesitated. He had said nothing but the idea of taking Jennifer Fair did not appeal to him. She was a responsibility and he shirked such things by nature. "Think we oughtta?" he asked. "Look, Colonel, I think—"

"She's going," Kimbrough said flatly. "Get on down there now."

Webb left, swearing to himself. "Think he was my bloody commandin' officer!" he muttered.

Zimmerman was ready . . . almost. There was one thing he wanted, and one thing he intended to have. He wanted the saddlebags Big Maria had brought into camp. Right now he was out in the rocks at the edge of the area, working around to the place where those bags must have been cached. Like Logan Cates, he had seen Maria slip away from the camp and hide them, and he had his own idea where they were. What was more, he was quite sure where they had come from.

For the past years Zimmerman had been thinking about that gold himself. A prisoner at Fort Yuma had whispered to him the story about the gold at the mines at Quitovac and had told him how easy it would be to get. The whispered information had been a bribe to escape, and Zimmerman let him go . . . and then shot him dead.

The mine was not far south of the border. There was one American there and four or five peons. A tough man or couple of men could handle it alone if nobody had an idea what they came for, and Zimmerman had been planning just that. Now he was quite sure that it was just this gold Big Maria had, and he wanted it.

Grant Kimbrough stooped over Jennifer and touched her

shoulder. Almost at once, her eyes opened. "Jen," he whispered, "come on. We're going!"

She sat bolt upright. "Going? Where?" She swept the sleeping camp. "Oh? You're going with Cates?"

"Cates?" he was puzzled. Jennifer had overheard a few words about the planned foray, and she had immediately surmised this was what he planned. "He has nothing to do with this! Come on, we're riding to Yuma!"

"Grant! You don't mean it! You'd leave . . . you'd desert them all?" Then she remembered. "Grant, aren't you supposed to be on guard?"

"Are you going to argue?" He was growing angry. "Let Cates hold these people if he wants to! I tell you, Jen, they'll all be killed, and we will too if we don't get out! Come on, your horse is saddled."

She got out from under her blanket and stood up. She thought of Yuma, of a town, houses, people, safety. Then she said something she would never have believed she could say. "I'm not going, Grant. I'm staying here."

He stared at her, coldly furious. What fool idea was this? "Jen," he began patiently, "you don't understand. Cates hasn't a chance of getting these people out of here alive; they're trapped, and he knows it. But all of us aren't so foolish as to stay; we're going out, and in a few hours we'll be safe in Yuma."

She hesitated. The camp around her was still. She could not see Cates, but he could be no more than a few yards away. It would be so easy . . . a swift ride over the darkening desert and they would be free, away from this and riding toward Yuma, marriage, and the world of cities, of ladies and gentlemen, of afternoon teas and pleasant, idle chatter.

It was what she wanted, and after all, what did these people mean to her? What could they mean? Logan Cates was a footloose cowhand—or worse, a man as like her father as another man could be. And who were the others? Such people as she had occasionally passed in the street, but nobody she would ever have known but for this.

"You'll have to hurry, Jennifer," he said. "We're all ready. Webb and Zimmerman are going with us."

She started forward, then stopped. "You go ahead, Grant. I'll stay here."

He was really angry. "Jen, don't be foolish! Why should you stay? These people mean nothing to you, and there will be more food and water for them! After all, it gives them a better chance, too."

"I'll stay here, Grant. Somebody will have to stand guard until they awaken. You go ahead."

"Without you?"

She looked up at him. "Yes, without me."

"But we're going to be married! We're engaged! It's only a few miles to Yuma."

"I'm sorry, Grant. You go ahead. If you make it to Yuma, send somebody for us. There will be time enough to talk of it then."

He stared at her, trying to stifle his fury. Without her there was nothing . . . nothing at all but going back to the gambling houses and the life he loathed. Yet what had she said? *Send somebody for them.* That was it. He could get help, come back, rescue them in the nick of time.

"Jen," he insisted, "you must come. There's no time to talk now. Come with me and we'll get the Army to come back here, and I'll come with them, but I want you out of here. I want you safe."

"I'm staying," she said quietly. "I'm not leaving until we can all go."

Zimmerman, only some thirty yards away, had reached the crevice where he was sure the gold would be. He reached into it and his fingers touched the cold leather of the saddle-bags. He grasped the top. His heart gave a leap—they were heavy, very heavy! They were bigger sacks than usual, obviously made for the purpose. He hauled them into the open and stood up.

Grasping the heavy bags he turned and stepped back into

101

the edge of the outer light from the fire. He took one more step, then froze. Behind him he heard the double click of a cocking shotgun . . . the double-barreled gun of Big Maria.

"Drop them bags, Zimmerman," Maria's voice was utterly cold. "Drop 'em or I'll cut you in two."

Zimmerman stood stockstill and helpless. Never for an instant did he doubt that she would kill, nor did he have any doubt she had already killed for the gold in the sacks. "Now look here," he said, trying to speak reasonably, "we can—"

"Drop 'em, mister."

He dropped them. Webb was staring at him over a saddle. Grant Kimbrough and Jennifer Fair had turned to face him, and beyond them, standing in the shadow at the far edge of the area, was Logan Cates.

Zimmerman turned around slowly. The shotgun was right on his belt buckle and it gave him a queasy feeling. A pistol he might face, a man had a chance there, but nobody had a chance against the twin barrels of a shotgun.

"Split fifty-fifty and I'll take you with me," Zimmerman said.

"You won't take her anywhere," Logan Cates said, his voice cutting across the night, "because you're not going anywhere."

Webb had heard enough. Zimmerman with his greed and Kimbrough with that girl, and now they'd missed their chance, but he had not! With a leap he was in the saddle, his spurs slapped home, and the zebra dun sailed over the lower rocks with a great bound and was gone in the night.

They were all up and standing around now. For a moment they listened to the rush of pounding hoofs.

"He won't get far," Cates said. "He's on my horse."

"What difference does that make?" Beaupre asked.

"I know that dun. He was startled by the sudden jump into the saddle but right now he knows what has happened."

The dun was running freely and Webb's heart was pounding wildly. He was away! He was free! He was—

The zebra dun felt the strange rider. He slowed, then suddenly braced his legs. Webb came loose in the saddle and caught himself, but not in time to save him as the dun swapped ends twice and sent him sailing. He hit the ground all in a heap and the dun's flying hoofs narrowly missed his skull, and then the dun was off into the night.

Webb lunged to his feet and started to cry out, then the danger of his position came home to him.

He was on his feet with only a pistol, and no horse, no canteen. There were Indians all around him.

He stood still for a moment. He could go back. He thought of that, then changed his mind. No, he was free. No matter what they said, it could not be far to water, and he would keep going. If the Apaches could live out in this desert, he could. He faced northwest and started walking.

Suddenly he seemed to hear something out in the desert. He paused, listening. He heard no sound. After a moment he walked on, and heard it again. He started to walk faster, then broke into a run. He ran and ran, then stumbled and fell. He scrambled to his feet, his hands bleeding, and rushed on. He plunged into a bunch of cholla, backed off filled with thorns and ran on . . .

At daylight, staggering with weariness, he was out on the desert. Not far away were some rocks. He started toward them. After an hour he was no nearer and the sun had come out. He stopped to try to pull thorns from his hands with his teeth. He pulled one out, then fastened his teeth in another. Something moved near him and he lifted his eyes to look.

For an instant he stared, then slowly his eyes went from right to left around him. He backed off a little, then turned, his teeth still in the thorn. They were all around him. There was no escape.

It was almost noon when they heard the first scream.

Kimbrough came to his feet, his face white with shock. "What was that?"

Nobody said anything for a long minute and then Cates replied, "That was Webb . . . he didn't like it here."

103

*   *   *

The dun came back shortly after noon. He came trotting in, stirrups flopping. Logan Cates walked to him and the dun jerked up his head, eyes rolling. Cates spoke to him softly, got hold of the bridle and led the horse to water. Then he unsaddled him and picketed him with the rest, gathering mesquite beans for him from places the horse could not reach. The screams had been coming for the past hour, but now they were growing fainter.

Nobody had said anything for a long time. Zimmerman walked over to Cates finally. "What are they doing to him?" he whispered hoarsely. His face was gray with horror and sweat beaded his brow. "He—he sounds like an animal."

"He is," Cates said dryly. "He's just a hurt animal, in pain. By now he doesn't even remember he was a man. I don't know what they're doing, maybe skinning him little by little, maybe sticking cholla thorns into him and setting fire to them. An Apache has a sight of imagination when it comes to that sort of thing."

Zimmerman mopped a big hand over his face. "You—you think we've got a chance, Cates?"

"We're alive, aren't we? Sure, we've got a chance."

The planned attack on the Indian camp had been given up, yet he knew it was still the thing to do, and might be their only chance to cut the odds between them. They had a man less now.

Taylor was staring at the saddlebags. "What's in them?" he asked.

"None of your business!" Big Maria flared.

Zimmerman squatted on his haunches. "I'll tell you what's in 'em," he said. "It's gold. Maybe sixty, seventy thousand dollars. And it's stolen gold, too."

"Stolen?"

"Yeah. My guess is from the mines at Quitovac. All that stuff about Tucson is a cock-an'-bull story. She was there, sure. But my guess is she an' her man went down to Quitovac after that gold. Prob'ly murdered old Adam down there."

"Ma'am," Taylor spoke sharply, "you'll have to turn that gold over to me. I am an officer of the law."

Big Maria's fat face was sweaty and dust-streaked. One stocking was down and her clothes were all awry, but there was no nonsense about the shotgun. "All right," she said, "you want it, you come an' get it."

Taylor wet his lips with his tongue. He stared greedily at the sack, but he made no move to get it at that particular moment.

"You don't have to go after it now," Zimmerman scoffed. "Just wait . . . whoever lives through this can ride out of here a rich man."

"That's enough of that talk!" Cates interrupted. "You have enough trouble without stirring it up among you. Zimmerman, you start any more of that talk and I'll send you out there after Webb."

Big Maria held her shotgun and stared defiantly at them, but Logan Cates ignored her. They were in trouble now. Webb would be tortured until he could stand no more, but once he was dead they would be liable to attack.

Sheehan came to him. He looked gray and old. "Sorry, Logan; sorry Webb went haywire on you. That comes from taking men into the Army who don't want to soldier. Zimmerman's the same . . . he was in trouble back East, joined up to get away from the law."

Taylor stalked over to them. "Cates, you order that woman to turn that gold over to me. I'm an officer of the law."

Logan Cates turned sharply around. "Taylor, you're a businessman who was deputized to join a posse, that's all. Out here you're not even that, you're a man who's fighting for his life. How she got that gold or what she does with it is none of my affair. My only concern is getting us out of here alive, if I can."

"When we get out of this," Taylor said maliciously, "I'm going to have the law check your background, Cates. You ride with the wrong herd."

"Oh, shut up!" Cates was disgusted. "Go on back and get your rifle. You'll be lucky if you don't wind up head down over a fire, like Webb probably did."

FOURTEEN

A hot wind blew dust across the clearing and sifted a thin film of it over the water in the pools. The water was low now; only a little remained. The sun was high, and from up in the rocks Beaupre watched the desert with eyes weary from staring over the hot sand. He felt worn out and tired, and for the first time he felt old. His had been the tireless strength built of long use, accustomed to hardship, scarce food and little water, and in the past he had never known what weariness could mean. Now he was bone-tired.

Logan Cates checked his Winchester. He looked across at Jennifer. She was strangely silent this morning, had gone about helping with the little food there was left, but said almost nothing. Junie sat close to Lonnie, and they were talking together. Grant Kimbrough sat alone.

Since the events of the previous night had become common knowledge, Cates had said nothing to Kimbrough. He had never liked the man, but he had believed he would stay put and fight; now he knew this was not so. Yet Grant Kimbrough was no coward, he was simply a selfish man—and such a man can be dangerous.

Taylor was greedy. He was more concerned with the gold

106

Big Maria had than with defending the rocks. He could not be depended upon.

Jennifer brought Cates a cup of coffee. "It's almost the last," she said, "and more than half mesquite bean, but it's all we have."

He grinned as he accepted it, and she thought again how tireless he seemed. "You've done nothing but think of us," she said. "You're the only one who has, unless it's the sergeant here."

"I want to get out alive."

"It's more than that."

"You know it is, ma'am." Sheehan glanced at her. "You stick with him, no matter what comes. If anybody can take care of you, he can."

"You probably think I'm a fool," she said, after Sheehan had gone. "I'm beginning to see what you meant about the kind of men it takes for this country."

"That boy your father killed," Cates said. "I know all about that. They called him Rio, didn't they?"

"Yes."

"He was a gunman . . . a killer for pay. They sent him to kill your father."

Her eyes searched his. "You're not just saying that to make it easier for me?"

"A man's worse than a fool who'll lie at a time like this," he said, "but you can ask Beaupre or even Taylor. Everybody on the border knows that story. Rio was from El Paso, and a bad man to tangle with. Friends tried to get your father to hire a gunfighter, but he told them he had always scotched his own snakes, and he was too old to change."

"I've been an awful fool."

"Who hasn't? A lot of people have to learn that a laughing boy isn't always a nice boy. I've seen Rio, he looked very gay and debonair in the saddle or afoot, and he had no more heart than a rattler."

She was silent. "Logan, I want to go back. I want to go back to my father."

"He'd like that."

"Will you take me back?"

His eyes searched hers. "If we get out of here," he promised, "I'll take you back."

A boot grated on gravel. "Running out on me, Jen?" Grant Kimbrough stood facing them. She thought again, in that moment, how the desert had a way of stripping the tinsel off things; it took rawhide and iron to stand up in the desert. "You won't get away with it, Jen. And Logan isn't taking you anywhere."

"We can talk about it later," Cates said mildly. "We've trouble enough."

Kimbrough laughed sarcastically. "Is that always the way you dodge trouble, Cates? I've heard you say that to Taylor, Zimmerman and Maria. Always the same thing. You knew that I planned to leave last night; why didn't you come to me and speak your piece? Were you afraid, Cates?"

"Afraid?"

"I've shot a crow on the wing, Cates." Kimbrough was smiling. "With one shot."

"Did the crow have a gun?" Cates asked gently. Kimbrough's smile vanished and Cates added, "I'll not be on the wing, Kimbrough, but I'll have a gun."

Sheehan had walked up silently, and now he glanced at Cates. "You're in the middle, boy, right in the middle of a target."

It was very hot. Dust blew across the clearing and stirred the sand on the desert. Logan Cates climbed back into the rocks and sat very still, trying to steady himself. It was getting him, too. The heat, the eternal watchfulness, the trouble within and without. Grant Kimbrough was very sure of himself with a gun . . . surer than any man would be who had not been successful. Kimbrough was positive he could beat Cates, and probably equally positive about anyone else.

He was a dangerous man, and especially dangerous now that he was close to the end of the tether. Out here, away from the eyes of the public, a lot could happen. Logan Cates had not missed the comment that the gold belonged to anyone who survived, nor had Kimbrough missed it. He would be thinking of that now, and he could no longer count on Jennifer Fair.

Taylor, Zimmerman and Kimbrough all felt themselves his enemies. Nobody knew where Beaupre or Lugo stood.

They moved out to the edge of the rocks and settled in place. It was going to be a long day, and the last of the food was gone. Only a little water was left. And out there in the desert, Webb had died screaming, his screams still ringing in the ears of those who defended the little circle of rocks.

Logan Cates searched the horizon, but a veil of dust and heat was drawn across the distance. Nothing was visible, but the sand, the sky, and the hard-boned ridges that thrust their serrated combs against the heat-misted horizon. The horses stood with heads down. Jim Beaupre got down from his place in the rocks and paced restlessly, his eyes searching the rocks as if looking for some escape.

Big Maria hunched over her saddlebags, half crazed by heat, greed, and the fear that somebody would deprive her of her wealth. Zimmerman scarcely looked at her. He had lost weight, looked thinner and somehow meaner and more vicious.

Only Lugo remained unchanged. He squatted among the rocks and wet the edge of the cigarette with his tongue. He glanced from time to time at Beaupre.

Sheehan was high in the rocks, searching for something at which to shoot. Suddenly, Cates saw him lift his rifle, a repressed eagerness in his manner. The muzzle eased forward between two rocks, the stock nestled against his cheek.

When the shot sounded, Cates thought for an instant that the sergeant had fired. Then Sheehan turned slowly around and let go his rifle. He fell then, fell from the rocks to the edge of the pool. He got up and took two staggering steps forward, then fell face down on the sand.

Cates ran to him, and when he turned him over there was no question. Sergeant Sheehan was dead.

"That's one less, Cates," Kimbrough said. "Brings you a little closer to the end."

"It brings us all closer."

Cates gathered up the rifle, then checked Sheehan's pockets for ammunition.

"Logan!" It was Lonnie Foreman. "They're comin'!"

They scrambled into position, yet the desert was empty. Suddenly as Foreman pointed, indicating a mesquite, Cates saw the brush move with a movement not of the wind. He swung his Winchester and fired three times, rapid fire, searching the bush with carefully spaced shots.

Lugo fired once, then again. On the far end, overlooking the arroyo, both Kimbrough and Taylor fired. There was a momentary silence brought to an end by Beaupre. The old skinner was suddenly on his feet, emptying his Winchester '73 into the brush. He fired rapidly, all seventeen bullets, smashing his shots into every bit of cover. Then he shifted position, loading swiftly. Leaping to the rocks, he smashed bullets at the edge of the dunes, running from place to place and firing as he ran from each pause. He fired into every available bit of cover, his shots ricocheting off rocks into concealed places or smashing into the brush.

"Jim!" Cates yelled at him above the sound of firing. "Get down! *Down!*"

Beaupre was up on the rocks. He fired; then, seeming to detect a movement, he swung swiftly about and fired at the base of a saguaro cactus. A burst of firing came from out front and Beaupre's body jerked, turned half around and fell back inside.

Cates ran to him. Beaupre's eyes flickered. "I had to do it, Logan," he said hoarsely. "I couldn't take it any longer. You—you take care of Tony. He's a good Indian."

"Jim!" Cates begged. "Hang on, man!"

Beaupre's eyes seemed to veil over. "Sorry—sorry, boy. Watch your back. You just watch your back."

Cates looked up to find Jennifer standing beside him. Cates got up slowly. "What did he mean by that?" she asked.

Whatever else Jim Beaupre had done, he had broken the attack. As though his death had brought death to the Apaches, silence descended upon the desert. Nothing moved, nothing made a sound, only the sun remained the same. It was hot, hot.

"Think he hit anything?" Lonnie asked.

"Maybe. I think so. It was good fire, right into all the cover there was. We'll never know."

Lonnie looked at him. "You don't think we'll get out?"

Cates shook his head. "No . . . suddenly I've a hunch we'll make it, or some of us will. Only you never know about Apaches. They carry their dead away. You never know if you've killed one or not, unless you kill them all."

"Six gone," Lonnie said. "Six good men."

Jennifer came over beside Cates and crouched down beside him. He turned to look at her. "Do you have a mirror?"

"A mirror?" Her eyes searched his. "Do you mean I should look at myself? I know I must be—"

"No, I want a mirror, the larger the better."

"There's one among my things, but—"

"Get it. Then you and Junie take turns. I want you to flash that mirror toward that peak over there"—he pointed toward the northeast—"and in that direction"—he indicated the northwest—"and I want you to travel the reflection between the two places. I want you to start now, relieve each other, and continue all through the daylight hours. Understand?"

"You mean to signal? We're signaling?"

"We hope you are," he pushed his hat back. "By this time there should be an armed force out. Maybe your father, maybe the Army, maybe a bunch of civilians and soldiers out of Yuma. They won't be expecting us to be this far south, and maybe there won't be anyone close enough to see your mirror, but I know a mirror can be seen for miles, even the sunlight on a bright concha. We'll try, and we'll hope."

"My mirror is not small," Jennifer said. "I have a special pocket in my saddlebag for it. Father had it made for me, and the mirror, too. It's a steel mirror, and is six-by-eight."

"Good! That's better than I'd hoped."

111

"Logan." She waited beside him. "Why couldn't we have done this before? We may be too late."

"Maybe, but I don't think so. Look, the way I've had it figured it would take several days for them to realize there's been trouble over this way. Maybe it was sooner, but probably several days. The same is true of Yuma. At first they wouldn't be worried when the posse didn't come back, or the soldiers. But as the days went by, they would be.

"It would take a while for them to agree that something should be done. Some are always for delaying, believing the people would come in, but by now they're sure something is wrong. Allow them two to three days out of either place to get here, and allowing for all that would have to happen before they get started and I think the time is now, and from now on."

"All right."

When she left him he studied the desert. He let his eyes sweep across it from close up to far out, then began searching the area with painstaking sweeps of his eyes across the terrain. When that was over he began to search the hills with his field glasses. Yet when half an hour had passed, he gave up.

Several times during the day haphazard arrows were fired into the camp, and twice there were shots, but no harm was done.

It was midafternoon when Kimbrough, Zimmerman and Taylor approached him. He had shifted back from his position to stretch his legs and have a drink of water. They walked up, Kimbrough in the lead.

"Cates, we want to make a run for it. We've horses enough now, and we think we can get through. At least some of us can."

"Sorry."

"Look, Cates," Kimbrough said roughly, "we've had enough of this. If we stay here they'll pick us off one by one. We'd rather make a fight of it."

"Kimbrough," Cates said slowly, "that route north out of here is called the Camino del Diablo—the Devil's Highway, if you prefer English. The only water on it is at Tinajas Altas, some tanks in the rocks of a ridge above the trail. Hundreds of men have died there, some of them within a few feet of the water. If you're lucky you'd find water when you get there, covered with green scum, maybe, but water. Only sometimes the tanks are empty. What do you do then?"

"We can make it."

"Sorry. Besides," Cates added, "we're still one horse shy. We have eight horses and nine riders."

Zimmerman swung his rifle. "I'll fix that, an' quick!" He lined his sights on Lugo, who was watching out across the desert.

"You drop that gun." Lonnie Foreman was sitting among the rocks, the Winchester in his hands trained on Zimmerman. "You drop it or I'll kill you!"

Zimmerman dropped his gun to the ground, swearing bitterly.

Grant Kimbrough had his hand negligently near his pistol. "Does somebody else always do your shooting for you, Cates? Seems to me the last time it was a girl."

"I knew Lonnie would take care of Zimmerman," Cates said mildly. "I was waiting for you."

Grant Kimbrough's face grew very still. His eyes widened just a little. His hand was very near the gun, and he had only to draw.

Logan Cates waited for him, the same mild expression on his face, his eyes smiling a little.

Kimbrough dropped his hand and turned away, and Cates looked after him. Kimbrough was not afraid, that Cates knew. The man was no coward, but Foreman was up there with a rifle and Cates was sure that Kimbrough believed that if he shot Cates, Lonnie would in turn kill him.

From the rocks nothing was visible. Shots kept coming, and the Indians were out there. Taylor tried two shots during the afternoon, but his eyes kept swinging to where Big Maria sat with her gold. Nobody had gone near her, nobody had spoken to her. Her heavy features looked dull, only her eyes

113

seemed alive. She had not left the money even for a drink. Whenever anyone moved, the shotgun followed.

During the last light of evening Logan Cates made a round of their defenses. If there were still enough Indians out there a rush might sweep over them and wipe them out. Yet the Indians might have suffered, too. He thought of Churupati . . . even his own people said he was insane, that his medicine was bad, and they would have nothing to do with him. He remembered the descriptions of the black-browed warrior, of the killings he had committed, the deaths for which he was responsible.

Some of the Indians had died, certainly more than they realized. Once that very morning he had sat trying to count up the possibilities, and they made an imposing array. The defenders were all good shots, and though few good targets had appeared, some of the searching fire would have scored.

The night came on and the wind began to blow again, and when the heat was gone the desert was cold. The wind was piercing, blowing through them, sapping the warmth from their bodies. They built a small fire and took turns warming themselves.

Cates went to the tank and dipped up a drink. When he finished he glanced at Maria, then suddenly dipped the cup deep and straightening, started toward her. Somebody said something in an undertone, and Kimbrough looked sharply around. Cates walked on, and Maria shifted the shotgun to cover him.

"Stay back."

It was the first thing she had said in hours. Cates continued to walk, holding the cup in front of him. "You need a drink, Maria," he said calmly, "and I'm bringing it to you."

"Stay back!" There was rising panic in her voice.

He walked up to her and handed her the cup. She looked up at him, then accepted the cup while keeping her right hand on the trigger guard of the shotgun. She drank thirstily, and then handed the cup back to him, her eyes never leaving his. Deliberately, he turned his back and walked away from her.

"She might have killed you!" Jennifer was horrified, aghast.

"She didn't," he replied.

"Mr. Cates." It was Junie. She was up in the rocks with Beaupre's rifle. "Mr. Cates, I think I can see a fire."

FIFTEEN

Logan Cates scrambled up into the rocks, and in an instant all with the exception of Big Maria were staring off toward the northeast in the direction Junie was indicating.

Nothing showed but the long line of mountains, dark blue with the late evening, shadowing to black where they met the desert. Only the mountains, the sky with the last of lingering day, the few stars showing their faces shyly against the backdrop of distance, and the sentinel saguaros nearby. Only the cholla seemed to hold a faint glow of their own; only these things, and nothing more.

They waited, and then they saw it, they all saw it, and they saw it at once. It was miles away, it was well up the mountainside, and it was definitely a fire.

"Who would want a fire that big?" Lonnie wondered.

"It doesn't have to be big," Cates told them. "On a night like this if it's high enough, a man can see a campfire for miles. They may be more than ten miles off; fact is, they are closer to fifteen."

"It's white man's fire," Lugo said. "No Indian build big fire."

"So," Taylor said, "what good does it do us?"

"If they can build a fire that we can see," Cates said, "we

116

can build one they can see. Only we've got to build up on the rocks."

"Anybody going near it will be a target," Taylor objected.

"We can feed it from below. We can poke sticks into it while staying out of sight. We can build the fire on that flat rock." He indicated a rock right behind where the man on watch always stood. "And I'll build it. Rustle wood, all of you."

There were a few sticks left where the fire had been and he gathered them up and carried them to the rock. It was the highest rock around, and it was shoulder-high to a standing man where one stood. Gathering the sticks he hurried back, placed them in order, and then with some crumpled leaves, a piece of cloth torn from his shirttail and some smaller sticks, he got the fire going. Then, reaching up from a crouching position, they added sticks to the fire.

The flames crept along the sticks, crackled and took hold. The flames leaped up, and each one vied with the others in running to carry wood to the fire. Soon a great, roaring flame lifted into the sky. Sparks climbed and mounted like floating stars high into the sky. Under the brush there was more wood, old dried and gnarled sticks, blackened by sun and exposure. These were added to the flames.

Suddenly a shot struck the rock where the fire was burning and ricocheted wickedly across the clearing. A burst of firing followed, but they huddled under the rocks and waited. Then they crept out and began gathering more sticks. Lonnie ventured down into the arroyo and returned with a load of big sticks thicker than a man's arm.

Suddenly, Cates was astonished to see Maria come up, bearing an armful of wood. She dropped it, then went back for more. Suddenly, as she was walking back with wood, she looked around at Jennifer. "Jen," she said, "I think they will come for us."

Her voice was strangely soft, and Jennifer glanced wonderingly at Logan Cates.

They worked busily, and despite the shooting, kept the fire going. Logan got his Winchester and began to shoot back at the muzzle blasts from the brush. Once when he fired they heard a scream from the brush, and after that, silence.

The fire soared, building its gold and orange flames into a red-line spire against the dark sky. The clearing was lighted like day and the firing continued.

Far and away the distant fire winked against the mountain-side. Was it a friendly fire? Across the distance it seemed like a beacon that spoke of home, of friends, of escape for them, but the fire told them nothing more. Had their own fire been seen? Or did anybody care?

The shots were fired from close up now, and soon once more the defenders scattered around the perimeter, firing back into the darkness.

"Keep it up," Cates told Lugo. "If they don't see the fire, they may hear the shooting. This air is very clear."

Yet it was a forlorn hope, all of it was. And in the morning there would be fighting. It was in the cold, lonely hours before dawn that the fire at last died down. To a man they were dog-tired and beaten, and the day was still to come.

"They'll be afraid," Cates told them, "that somebody saw our signal. In the morning, come daylight, there will be Indians."

Suddenly Big Maria screamed. It was a hoarse, choking scream. They turned swiftly to look, and Zimmerman was backing away from them, and he had the saddlebags. In his hand he held a big Colt. He was grinning.

"Wherever that fire is," he said, "there's people. And where people are, that's where I want to be."

"Give her back the gold," Cates told him. His face was suddenly icy. "Drop it, Zimmerman, and get away from it."

"Like hell!" Zimmerman was backing toward the horses, and now they saw that one of them was saddled. "You stay if you want to. I'm ridin' out!"

He was watching Cates and grinning, and his Colt was right on Cates's belt line. He was watching Cates and the others as he backed away, and there was in his mind no other thing than the fact that he had the gold, that he would take a horse.

Cates watched him and waited for the break he was sure would come. But Zimmerman was much too careful. He had kicked Maria's shotgun out of the way, and they all knew he would kill. Still facing them, he stepped into the stirrup and swung into the saddle. He remembered them, he gave them no chance at all, but he forgot to keep his head down. Even as the horse gave the first jump there was a shot from somewhere out beyond the rocks and Zimmerman stiffened with shock. The horse made it over the rocks into the sand as Zimmerman toppled from the saddle, his foot caught in the stirrup.

For a few yards the horse dragged him, then the hastily cinched saddle slipped and the horse stopped, the fallen man's foot still caught in the stirrup of the saddle which had slipped sidewise.

Taylor rushed to the rocks. "The gold! We've got to get that gold!"

"To hell with the gold," Cates said. "We need the horse."

Taylor started through the rocks. "Come back, you fool!" Cates yelled at him. "They'll get you, too!"

Taylor was beyond thinking. He hesitated only an instant, then sprang in the open. He ran down the slight incline through the sand and rushed up to the standing horse. The animal shied a little, but Taylor dropped on his knees in the sand and began tearing at the saddebags.

Cates, Kimbrough and Lonnie watched to cover him with rifle fire if any attempt was made to reach him. Lugo watched from the opposite side, and Junie stood close beside him, holding Beaupre's rifle.

Taylor was frantic. He jerked the saddlebags free; then instead of trying to return, he ripped loose the girth and sprang bareback on the horse. Booting it in the ribs, he started off.

"The damn fool!" Cates stood back wearily. "He's trying to get away!"

The horse was running like a frightened rabbit, and Kimbrough swore softly. "He's going to make it, too! He's getting away!"

In the open desert the horse was running beautifully,

119

when they heard the shots. Not one or two shots, but a ragged volley. Taylor was swept from the saddle as if by a mighty blow. He hit the sand, slid a few feet, then stopped. Suddenly he was on his feet, and, still holding the sacks, he started to run, and this time he ran back toward them while the horse, holding his head high, ran in a small circle and stopped, looking back.

Taylor was running desperately. Now that he was too far away he seemed bent only on getting back to the circle of rocks at Papago Wells.

"He's going to make it!" Lonnie said.

"No." Logan Cates shook his head. "He hasn't a chance. They're letting him come. Churupati is just having fun." Jennifer stared at him, shocked. "It's true," Cates said, "he hasn't a chance."

Yet Taylor ran on. He seemed inexhaustible. He ran to the very foot of the slight slope until he was almost close enough for them to see his features. Then he stumbled and fell in the soft sand. He staggered to his feet, then stared down. The saddlebags had come open and had spilled out nothing but sand and fragments of rock!

Taylor seemed frozen. He stared, unwilling to believe what his eyes told him. Then he turned his head and looked up at the wall of rocks, standing very still.

Suddenly frantic with unbelief, he picked up the other saddlebag and ripped it open, emptying it out, and nothing came but fragments of lava rock and a little sand. He seemed to come to himself with a start, and for the first time he realized that he was standing still, out in the open, that there was nobody anywhere around and that shelter was all of sixty yards away.

He dropped the useless saddlebags and started to run. It was a clumsy run now, but he ran, and from the rocks they could see his face straining with the effort he was making. He ran up the slope, seemed almost about to make it, and then there were three quick shots and he pulled up stiffly, turned halfway around and fell back, rolling over and over to the bottom of the slight slope.

Big Maria pointed her finger and screamed with wild, hysterical laughter. "The fool! You're all fools! Look!" She ran to the rocks and hauled from them the strip of canvas ground sheet that had covered her bedroll when she rode in. "Did they think I was crazy? I switched the gold, and the fools were killing themselves over a sack of old rocks!" She went off into screams of wild laughter.

Jennifer stared at Maria, appalled. Cates took her arm and turned her away. "She's insane," he said. "She's completely insane."

Lugo fired suddenly and they heard the flat, ugly impact of the bullets. He waited a moment, then fired another shot, holding a little lower. The bush moved as though tugged by hands, then was still. The wind stirred the sand along the ground, and that was all.

"Logan," Jennifer whispered, "I think I see some dust . . . it's still very far off."

They looked. Was it the dust of riders or a tiny whirlwind, the dust-devil of the desert? Or was it a trick of the dancing heat waves? They stared until their eyes tired from the strain and they saw nothing more, nothing more at all.

Suddenly the shooting began again. Shots kicked up sand and ricocheted from the rocks. Cates ducked from point to point, trying a shot wherever movement showed or cover offered. It was like fighting shadows, yet they knew that the Apaches, if they managed to get into their small circle of defense, would wipe them out. A sudden rush could overwhelm the defenders and their only hope was to send searching fire into every possible cover and stop such an attack before it began.

Yet the firing slackened, and seemed less than before, and at the end only one or two rifles were working, and no arrows came at all. Then silence.

In the silence that followed the thunder of rifle fire, Grant Kimbrough looked into a desert as empty as his own hopes. All

121

his plans were destroyed. Jennifer was a beautiful girl and a wealthy one, a girl he could admire and a girl of whom he could be proud, yet suddenly she was lost to him, and without doubt it was Cates who was responsible.

Nothing awaited him but more gambling, the endless round of smoky saloons crowded with sweaty, whiskered, hard-pushing men, and ever and always the chance that some day he would draw a gun too slowly. Yet he had never drawn too slowly so far, and now it might be all there was left.

He considered that. The small party had dwindled until only a handful were left, and on the ground behind them lay nearly seventy thousand dollars in gold, a small fortune to a man who could go to San Francisco and invest it wisely. A small fortune that could grow into a great fortune. Nothing moved out there in the desert over which he looked.

Cates. Logan Cates was the trouble. Had it not been for him Jennifer and he might have gone on to Yuma. With Cates out of the way the entire situation might change. There was still time to talk to Jennifer, and the kids didn't matter. There was Lugo, but nobody paid any attention to an Indian, and Maria—if she was not insane now she was verging on it. Besides, this wasn't over and it would be only too easy for one or more of them to die before it was over.

The fire last night might mean something and might not, but one thing he did know—there were fewer Indians out there than there had been. He was sure he had killed at least one during the last burst of fire, and only a few shots had been fired from his side of the circle.

Cover was not too plentiful out there, not so much that a man could not see most of the places where attackers might be, and over the days a lot of firing had been done. At times the execution must have been frightful.

There comes a time in the life of each man when he must make a decision. Grant Kimbrough had made one such decision when he sold out and left his home after the war. He had made another when he gave up his trip to San Francisco and went home with Jennifer Fair. He had another one to make now: behind him on the sand was a small fortune. Behind him was a girl he wanted, but whether he got her or not, the gold was there. And all that stood in his way was the load carried by his six-shooter.

It was murder, but he had killed before this. What of the men who died during the war, and those Indians who died here? Suppose, just suppose nobody was left alive but himself? It could easily happen. For that matter they might all be killed, himself included. And if only one or two were left, well, who was to say how they died?

He stared bleakly at the sand. He had come a long way since the old days. He shied away from the memory of his father. He could see the old man now. If his father had ever believed his son capable of what he now considered his father would have killed him himself. Yet his father had never been in such a position; all that lay between himself and a bleak future was a few pistol bullets.

The silence held. Nothing moved out there, not even a dust devil. The sky was an odd color, somewhere far off dust was blowing. It had changed to a weird yellow, like nothing he had ever seen, and the sky overhead seemed somehow higher, vaster, emptier. Like a great hollow globe of that vast yellow.

Behind him he heard Logan Cates say, "Sand storm coming, and a bad one."

A sand storm . . . sand that buried tracks, buried people, wiped out the trails into the past and only left open the new trails, the one that led on from this place.

There was time. Kimbrough would wait a little longer.

SIXTEEN

And so the sun shone . . . and there seemed no end to its shining, but now the high dust carried by the winds above the mountains obscured the sun but took away no heat. It lay heavy upon the land, and although the heat waves were gone and the yellow pall covered the higher heavens, there was silence everywhere.

No birds flew . . . no lizard moved upon the ground . . . no quail called from the distant trees, for there was silence, and only silence.

There is upon the great sand wastes no more terrible thing than a sand storm . . . the driving grains of sand wipe out the earth and sky, obscure the horizons, and close one in a tight and lonely world no more than a few feet square. Until one has experienced a sand storm upon the desert one cannot know horror; until one has felt the lashing whips of sand one cannot know agony; and until one has felt that heat, that terror, that feeling that all the world has gone wrong, one has not known hell.

The birds cease to fly, the tiny animals, even the insects hunt their hidden places. Horses roll their eyes, wild with terror, and men find places to hide from the stifling dust. Yet it is not the wind, nor the sand, nor the heat alone; it is the terror, the frantic choking, the gasping, the struggle and the cowering fear brought on in part by the quivering electricity in the air, the unbearable tension, the loss of all perspective. Our senses are fragile things, dainty things, occasionally trustworthy, yet always demanding of perspective. Our senses need horizons, they need gauges, they need rules by which to apply themselves, and in the sand storm there is no horizon and there are no rules. There is no near or far, no high or low, no cold or warm, there is only that moving wall of wind that roars out of distance, screaming insanely, screaming and roaring. And with it the uncounted trillions of lashing sand bits. One moves at the bottom of a moving sea, a literal sea of sand, whose surface is somewhere high above in the great vault of the heavens, and one dies choking, crawling on the hands and knees, choking with sand, choking with wind, choking with the effort to breathe.

Such a storm was coming now.

Logan Cates knew it was coming. He felt electricity in the air prickle the hair on the back of his neck, he saw the sky weirdly lit, and he knew the storm was coming. The horses tugged and pulled, anxious to run, yet there was nowhere to run, nowhere to go.

Jennifer stared at him, wide-eyed and frightened. "What is it, Logan? What's happening? What's wrong? There's something strange."

"It's the storm." Cates turned swiftly. "Lonnie, Kimbrough, fill all the canteens, and make it fast. Lugo, hobble the horses, and get them down into the bottom."

"What about the Indians?" Junie asked.

"Don't think about them. They'll be having troubles of their own. Hurry!"

They worked swiftly, driven by a sort of panic, feeling the strange, vast stillness, feeling like tiny things at the bottom of a huge bowl. Of them all, only Cates and Lugo knew what they faced, and there is no worse thing than a sand storm in a desert of loose sand.

Vast dunes of it lay to the south of them, and there were

125

dunes to the west and north, and some to the east, vast quantities of loose sand awaiting the hand of the wind. Cates led the horses into the bottom of the arroyo, working with the Pima. Feverishly the others worked, filling the canteens. Maria sat stolidly, seemingly unaware . . . and at the last moment when the others had gone below, Cates came to her. "Come, Maria, we're going below."

She looked up at him with wide, liquid eyes. "No, not yet."

He hesitated, then turned away to carry a last canteen of water and an armful of hastily gathered wood from the remains of the big fire.

Grant Kimbrough came up through the rocks and looked quickly around. There was no one, only Maria, and she was staring at the vast yellow sky. Dropping swiftly to his knees, he scooped the gold into a heap and gathered it in handfuls to throw into the saddlebags he had hastily concealed in the rocks when carrying his saddle below. It was the work of a few seconds, and in that time Maria did not turn to look or give any evidence that she heard the faint, small sounds of his working. Quickly, he carried the saddlebags below and placed them near the mouth of the wind-hollowed, shallow cave that was their only shelter.

The cave offered only a few feet of overhang, and partial shelter from a clump of mesquite. Behind this clump they held the horses, tied tight against lunging.

Cates looked up suddenly and straightened to his feet, listening. There was a faint, far-off sound, a sound that as he listened grew into a vast and mammoth roaring. "It's coming," he said. "Get back against the rocks."

He started for the path to the upper arroyo. Jennifer ran after him. "Logan, no!"

He had to shout to make her hear, although the sand was still distant. "Maria!" he shouted.

Wheeling, he ran up the path and she followed, at the top they looked around. There was nobody, anywhere. Maria was gone!

Appalled, he sprang to the top of the rocks and looked quickly around. Then he pointed.

Jennifer stared in consternation and horror. At least two hundred yards away, walking south into the desert, was Maria. She was walking quietly along, her square and heavy figure, shoulders somewhat stooped, but carrying a dignity all her own, acting as if nothing more serious impended than an afternoon stroll. She walked steadily, plodding through the sand, headed south in the wild, unbelievable loneliness toward Pinacate and the Gulf.

Cates shouted, throwing his voice into the awful roar of the wind, but she could not have heard him. And if she did, by some freak of the wind, she did not turn or look back.

"Logan!" Jennifer cried. "We've got to get her! We must!"

"We couldn't!" he shouted. "There isn't time!" He pointed to the open desert. There, only a mile or two away, and roaring toward them, was a wall of sand that towered thousands of feet into the sky; before it tumbleweeds rolled and bounced, and before it came a strange chill, frightening after the heat of the earlier day.

Catching Jennifer's hand, he ran back to the path. Cowering to catch a breath in the shelter of some rocks, he shouted into her ear, "Think of it! What is there left for her? She'd be arrested for robbery, probably murder! It's better this way!" And he pulled her toward shelter.

They stumbled down into the hollow under the arroyo bank. And then the wind came.

Junie huddled close in Lonnie Foreman's arms, her coat wrapped about her, a blanket over her hair and face. Grant Kimbrough stared at them, his face expressionless, showing neither emotion nor feeling of any kind. He drew his hat down hard and turned up the collar of his frayed frock coat, gathering a blanket around him. Lugo huddled in a blanket of his own near the horses, only his eyes visible, and when Jennifer Fair cuddled into a blanket with Logan Cates neither he nor anyone was surprised. He held her close, feeling her warmth, knowing

127

suddenly this was the way it must be, not only now, but always.

And the wind blew.

It was like no other wind, it was like no other sound, it was a vast, mighty roaring, a sound beyond understanding that filled all the space between the mountains, and over them the sand blew, shutting them into their hollow, ripping shrubs from the earth, rolling stones that echoed down the wash with great, hollow, knocking sounds. Sand sifted into their eyes and ears, it choked their throats, and the air grew colder still, colder and thinner, until they gasped for every breath, fighting to stay alive, fighting to avoid suffocation.

All sense of time was lost; they clung to each other as drowning people cling, frightened, cold, and alone. The earth seemed to rock beneath them, and still they clung together, and after that, a long time after, when minds, nerves and bodies were too weary to stand any further strain, they slept.

Logan Cates awakened, chilled to the bone, to hear a faint stirring. He parted the blanket and sand cascaded from him. Huddled together as they were, they had been half buried in the blown sand. Tony Lugo was saddling a horse.

Cates got stiffly to his feet and began digging the firewood from the sand. "Going somewhere?" he asked.

"I think better I ride," Lugo said quietly. "Soon white men come." He twisted the rope in his hands. "Maybe they from Yuma."

"All right, Tony." He brought a twist of grass, hastily ripped up the night before, from his pocket. Thrusting it under the wood he cupped a match in his stiff fingers. The grass caught, then a bit of hanging bark, and soon a fire was crackling.

Then Tony Lugo's words penetrated.

"There are white men coming?"

The Pima nodded. "They far off, one, two hour. I see them."

Lugo paused as if searching for words, then glanced meaningfully at the still huddled shape of Grant Kimbrough. "Gold gone," he said.

"Covered with sand, probably."

"No."

Logan Cates considered that. Had there been a slight move from Kimbrough? Was the man listening? "No matter," he said. He glanced at Lugo. "Did you want it?"

If Lugo could have looked amused, he would have. "No, I have horse, gun, maybe two dollars, I get drunk. Man have gold, he runs too fast. All the time run fast before maybe somebody catch up." He stepped into the saddle. For a moment he hesitated. "You good man, Cates."

He put the horse up the path and was gone. Logan looked after him, then knelt to stoke his fire, and when he looked around, the others were stirring, getting out of their blankets. Jennifer brushed her hair back and went to the waterhole, then up the path to the others. She came back, running.

"Logan! The water's gone! It's all dried up and the holes are half full of sand!"

"I know. That's why I had the canteens filled. The air in those storms is so dry it sucks up any water that's left."

Grant Kimbrough folded his blanket and picked up his saddle. Jennifer glanced at him, then at Cates, who said nothing. Kimbrough saddled his horse.

Lonnie and Junie were folding the little gear there was left.

Jennifer stood over the fire, warming herself, and Logan Cates waited, spreading his fingers over the flames.

Kimbrough finished his saddling and turned on them.

"Why don't you say something, Cates? You know I got the gold. Why don't you say something about it?"

Logan Cates lifted his eyes. In that moment he knew that what was to come could not be avoided. He was glad that Jennifer was out of the line of fire, but wished she were further away. The kids against the back wall were all right.

"I don't say anything about it, Kimbrough," he said quietly, "because I don't care."

129

LOUIS L'AMOUR

"You don't care?"

"Why should I? It doesn't belong to me, and I don't want it. As far as that goes, it won't do you any good, either. If you stop and think about it, you know it, too."

"What do you mean by that?"

"You may have some bright ideas about investments, but that just won't be. You'll gamble it, lose a little, win a little, and finally lose it all."

Something inside Kimbrough died. Suddenly he knew that what Logan Cates had said was true. He would gamble it away, and if he had married Jennifer he might, sooner or later, have gambled that away, or let it waste. He knew it and hated Cates for making him know it.

"You're wrong, Cates," he said, and his voice sounded strange in the hollow of the bank. "You're wrong about that, and wrong about a lot of things. You believe you'll ride out of here with Jennifer, but you won't. Only one person is riding out of here, and that's me."

Logan Cates heard Lonnie turn slowly around, and hoped Lonnie would stay out of it.

Kimbrough said, "Don't look for your gun, kid. I've got it. I took it last night when the wind was blowing. I'd have taken yours, Cates, only you I want to kill."

"Grant! What are you saying?" Jennifer pleaded. "You can't mean that! Take the gold. We don't want it."

"How far would I get with it? Don't be a fool, Jen. I've thought it all out. That Indian won't talk, they never do, and I'll make sure the rest of you don't do any talking."

Kimbrough looked at Cates. "I've waited for this for a long time, and this time there won't be anybody to keep you from having to face the issue. This time nobody else has a gun."

Logan Cates stood very tall and still. He stood with his feet a little apart, waiting, simply waiting. "Kimbrough, in this like everything else, you're a tinhorn."

Kimbrough was very sure of himself. "What are you going to do, Cates, when I go for a gun?"

130

It was then they heard the horses. They heard a sound of hoofbeats, and someone called out loudly.

Kimbrough went for his gun and Logan Cates shot him.

It was that simple and that quick. Cates was firing before Kimbrough's gun came level, and his bullet smashed the gambler halfway around and the second bullet punctured his lungs from side to side. His gun went off into the sand, and he fell, face down and hard, the pistol flying from his grip. He tried to get up, an almost spasmodic effort, then fell back and rolled over.

"You . . . you beat me, Cates. You beat me."

Logan Cates looked down at him. "Sorry, Kimbrough. You should have known better. I was doing this when I was sixteen."

Grant Kimbrough tried to speak, then relaxed slowly, and he was dead. . . .

The riders came down the trail and drew up before the opening. Logan Cates looked up and knew at once that the big, gray-haired man was Jim Fair.

"Who're you?" Fair's voice rumbled. It was harsh, commanding.

"I'm Logan Cates," he replied shortly. "I'm the man who's marrying your daughter."

Jim Fair stared at him, his eyes hard. "All right, get on your horses and let's get out of here." Fair glanced around at Jennifer. "You all right, Jennifer?"

"I'm fine, Dad, but I want to go home."

Fair jerked his head at Cates. "Is this your man?"

"He is."

"You're a lot smarter'n you were," Fair said grimly. He glanced at Lonnie Foreman. "You punch cows?"

"Sure."

"You got a job."

After the horses had gone, the wind blew a light sifting of sand over the clearing, and that was all. The sand blew and exposed an arrowhead that lay there, an arrowhead that might have been a thousand years old. The wind blew, the sand sifted, and there was nothing more.

131

The waterholes at Papago Wells would fill again when the rains came, and others would come and some would live and some would die, but the Wells would always be there in the changing of years.

The sand sifted before the wind and somewhere out in the mesquite a quail called inquiringly into the night.